MERRY MISTLETOE

Sherbourne Mistletoe has been prized and sold at the annual Mistletoe Fair for over a century. But could this year possibly be the last? With her father's sudden death, and debts mounting up, it looks as though Freya's only hope for the future is to sell her beloved family home. Then the arrival of the mysterious Amos Fry brings a glimmer of hope — and Freya might just fall in love with Christmas all over again.

EMMA DAVIES

MERRY MISTLETOE

Complete and Unabridged

LINFORD
Leicester

First published in Great Britain in 2015

First Linford Edition
published 2021
by arrangement with
Bookouture
London

*A catalogue record for this book is available
from the British Library.*

ISBN 978–1–4448–4797–0

Published by
Ulverscroft Limited
Anstey, Leicestershire

Printed and bound in Great Britain by
TJ Books Ltd., Padstow, Cornwall

This book is printed on acid-free paper

For Peta, who first believed.

WINTER

1

Freya slammed the van door closed and leaned up against it, breathing hard, her breath appearing as sharp little puffs in the cold. How difficult could it be? After all, she'd done this countless times before. Except she hadn't, because this year she was alone.

She shivered in the harsh early morning air; whether from nerves or the cold, she couldn't tell, and, in any case, it hardly mattered, the effect was the same. She glanced back at the house, solid and warm and comforting, and tried to damp down the rising sense of panic that threatened to swamp her. She sucked in a breath and, resolutely ignoring the 'For Sale' sign, gave a little nod in farewell. Whatever happened today she was going to give it her best shot; she owed her dad that much after all.

The weather forecast was clear, the very best kind of day. Cold, but with a defiant blue sky that not only cheered the gathered crowds but brought a strong contrast to the holly berries and a gleam to the glossy leaves. She'd dressed for the part too, in her forest green coat and bright red woolly hat and scarf that always made her feel much warmer than she was. The colour brought a rosy hue to her cheeks and made her chestnut hair glow. The punters seemed to like it too. Christmas was just over a month away, and if it helped to look like Mrs Claus, then who was she to argue.

She edged the van out of the gate and onto the lane, reminding herself to breathe normally. It was important to get there early, but she had plenty of time to secure a good spot, and the roads would be relatively quiet at this time of the morning. In an hour's time, she'd make it to Tenbury Wells and could stop fretting.

The familiar landmarks came and went. Freya knew the route like the back of her hand, and, three miles in, she began to feel the first bubbles of excitement welling up inside her. She had first travelled this route over twenty-five years ago when she was just a girl, and every year since, she and her dad had made the journey to the annual mistletoe sales. Her granddad had been there before them too for many a year, and even as a small child, she remembered his tales. Sherbourne mistletoe had been sold at the fair for nearly a hundred years all told, and the thought that this might be her last ever year sat like a stone in her stomach. There would be enough time to think about that though, in the weeks to come; today she had to hold her head high.

It was the boots that Freya noticed first: bright red Doc Martens. She'd never seen him wearing anything else, so maybe he didn't own any other shoes, but today, trudging along the muddy verge, they stood out in stark contrast to everything else. She hadn't seen him for a couple of days, but by the look of him, he was moving on somewhere. She slowed the van on the empty road and

5

pulled up alongside him.

'Amos?' she called.

He turned at the sound of her voice, breaking into a broad grin. 'Well, hello again, Miss Sherbourne, what brings you this way?'

She smiled. It was just the sort of thing he would say, as if it were she who was in the wrong place. 'Well, I live around here, but I don't know about you. And more to the point, you didn't even say goodbye.'

His black eyes twinkled. 'Ah well, you know that's not my style. Besides, I thought I'd finished everything you needed me to do.'

'You did, but it's nearly Christmas, Amos. I could have found a few other things for you. It's not a great time to be without a place to go.'

He dipped his head slightly in acknowledgement of her concern. 'But when I get where I'm going, I'll be someplace, won't I?' He squinted up at her through the sun. 'Anyhow, I think it was time for me to move on.'

Freya blushed slightly. 'Gareth was okay with you being around, really he was. He just . . . well, he likes things to be . . . ordinary.'

'And I offended his sensibilities, I understand that.'

'I don't think he understood you, that's all; the choices you've made.' She was trying to be tactful, knowing full well that Amos had heard at least one sarcastic comment that Gareth had made at his expense. Judging by the look on his face however, he understood Gareth's motives very clearly, and really Freya was in no position to argue. She had wanted to help, that was all, but she could also see it from her boyfriend's point of view. Maybe Amos' leaving was for the best.

'So where are you headed to now then?'

Amos surveyed the road ahead, his tight black curls gleaming in the sunshine. 'This way will do.'

'And when you get to the end of this way, where next?'

'Well now, see, that's the best bit. I'll

just go the way the wind blows me.'

Freya drummed her fingers on the steering wheel. 'There's a fair wind howling down the A49 today, I reckon. Have you ever been to the mistletoe fair?'

'Not that I can recall.'

'Well, seeing as you helped me to harvest it all, do you want to see what happens next?'

Amos looked at his watch, as though he had some pressing engagement. 'You might need some help then?'

'I might. And I'll buy you lunch and a pint when it's over.'

She leaned over to open the passenger door as Amos shrugged his rucksack off his shoulders. He climbed in, wedging his belongings on the floor of the cab, before taking a deep breath and inhaling the smell of the greenery from within.

'Magical stuff mistletoe,' said Amos. 'But I expect you know that. I've always thought it a rather wonderful coincidence that it appears at Christmas; it seems exactly the right time of year for a miracle or two, don't you think?'

Talk about cutting it fine, thought Amos. A few moments later and she might have missed him altogether, and then where would he be? Sometimes, he knew the minute he ended up in a place why he was there, and, sometimes, it took a while longer. This time had been the hardest of them all to call. He'd been in Much Marlowes since the beginning of August, and the jobs that took him there had both been straightforward. Two beautiful cottages rethatched, but no hint of any reason for him to stay. Ordinary families, settled lives, and not the slightest prickling feeling that usually alerted him to his purpose.

It wasn't until he pitched up at the Sherbourne orchard that he began to feel he might be onto something, although at the time he had wondered whether it was the after-effects of too much cider the night before. A drunken bet in a game of cards had cost him his van, and the only reason he had turned up

Freya's drive was the hope of quenching a raging thirst. As he walked its length, however, it occurred to him that the apple harvest might be his salvation, and when Freya opened the door, a wave of dizziness had passed over him so strong it had nearly taken him off his feet. He knew then without a shadow of a doubt that he would stay.

Several glasses of water later and two hours' sleep had allowed him to recover, and by then, Freya had already decided to offer him some work. She couldn't afford to pay him much, but he had food, a place to stay, and the weeks had slipped by. By the middle of October, however, he was none the wiser. Freya's boyfriend, Gareth, was a prize pillock but harmless enough, and although their relationship had clearly lost its sparkle (if it had ever had any), they rubbed along peaceably enough. There seemed no real reason for him to be there after all, and so helping her harvest the holly and mistletoe had been his final job. He must simply have been mistaken, and it was time for him to move on once more.

He knew it was her, though, the minute he heard the van slow down, and now as he sat in the warmth beside her, he found he was rubbing the back of his neck repeatedly to calm the prickling sensation he felt there. She had crossed his path again, and he wasn't sure what the mistletoe fair had to do with things, but there was no doubt in his mind that he had to find out.

With the radio playing all the way and the two of them singing songs at the top of their voices, the miles slipped by, so it was only when they turned down a road to join a convoy of other vans that Amos realised they must be close. He glanced at Freya, but she seemed relaxed enough, despite how he knew she must be feeling. She chatted easily to him when it was just the two of them; it was only the evenings when Gareth was around that she clammed up. But this fair meant a lot to her, he knew that much.

The auction yard was busy as they turned in, already milling with people and vehicles as the traders sought to find their spaces and unload their wares. Freya gave an explosive tut beside him.

'Bloody Hendersons,' she said. 'I might have known they'd get here before me.'

Amos followed the angle of her head to a smart lorry, its familiar red livery bright and distinctive in the morning sun. He'd seen them about the lanes quite often over recent weeks, and on the odd occasion when Freya mentioned their name, it was never in flattering tones.

'Look at him, pig-headed arrogant sod; thinks he owns the place.'

It was true that the lorry was now holding everyone else up as it manoeuvred into position, but there was still plenty of room for Freya's smaller van to pass. He glanced at the jut of her chin, deciding not to argue, and pointed out a place further along which she could easily fit into.

Freya was out of the cab in a flash, running over to the pens in a barn which ran along one side of the yard. He watched her walk up and down, her red scarf flying behind her, a coiled little bundle of energy. She paused every now and then before stopping completely, and with a visible little hop, spun on her heels and threaded her way hurriedly back towards him.

'Right, I'm good with that,' she said breathlessly. 'My pitch is right smack bang in the middle, just about perfect.' She grinned at the perplexed look he gave her. 'I'll explain later. Come on, we need to get over to where the rest of the sale takes place.'

She threw a look over to the Henderson's lorry before flinging open the back doors of the van and climbing inside. Amos lost her among the foliage for a second. A riot of green and red and silver greeted him. If you could capture Christmas in a single scene, this would surely come close. He'd really had no sense of it while he was helping her to cut it down, but now, bundled as it was and filling the space, it was a joyful homage to the season.

Freya threw him a pair of gloves as

the holly came out first, dark and gleaming. The plant he knew well, but he was certainly no expert on selling the stuff. It was full of berries, though, and he thought that could only be a good thing. She stopped for a moment, her head on one side like a robin, her eyes on his, suddenly anxious.

'Jesus, Amos, what am I doing?'

He really didn't have an answer but smiled in encouragement.

'How can I possibly compete with this lot? I mean look at them. They've easily three times as much as I have. No one's going to want my paltry few bundles. I shouldn't have come.'

Amos picked up a sheaf of the holly, holding it close to his body. He touched a round red berry gently and ran a finger down the spine of a rich dark leaf. 'But this is beautiful, Freya. I would buy it, if I could.' He was horrified to see her eyes begin to glisten. 'Have you been here lots of times before?'

She gave a small nod. 'Yes, but that was . . . was with my dad.'

'And would you feel like this if your dad were here today? Would you want to give up and go home?'

'No, of course not, but that was different.' She frowned. 'Things were different then.'

'Only if you believe them to be,' he said softly. He reached into the bundle and plucked a small white feather from its depths before taking her hand to help her down from the van. Gently placing the holly on the floor, he tucked the feather into the rim of her hat, pushing it into the woollen folds.

'There are always times when your father is with you, Freya, more often than you know.' He looked up to see her eyes widen in surprise. 'Now, since you're the expert here, can I suggest that you tell me where these need to go; I'm guessing that wherever it is, you'll want them there before the Hendersons?'

Her gaze wandered over his left shoulder just for a second before shooting back to him, her eyes still glistening but now with a new-found glint of determination.

She picked up a bundle, seemingly oblivious to the sharpness of the prickles, and, with a grin and a nod of her head, marched off, leaving Amos to trail in her wake.

Once the holly was laid out, they doubled back to the van to collect the mistletoe and began the same process all over again, laying out their bundles in tight little rows in the yard, while prospective buyers milled around, nodding and chatting in fine mood. Amos caught sight of one of them pointing to Freya's bundles, although he made no move to examine it further. He heard the name Sherbourne muttered and smiled to himself. Despite her reservations, her name had obviously preceded her, and her bright blue labels with their distinctive name stamp were doing their job brilliantly.

'I wasn't sure if you'd be here this year, but you made it then.'

Amos whipped around at the sound of the voice, its tone none too friendly.

Freya dipped her head. 'Hello, Stephen.'

The two of them stared at one another for a moment without saying anything further, but Stephen's gaze was travelling up and down the rows of mistletoe, resting on Freya's bundles for a moment too long to be comfortable.

'Berries looking a little green I'd say, Freya,' he said, smiling a smug grin.

His hair was slicked back into a quiff at the front, and a signet ring glistened on one of the fingers he was wiping across his smirking mouth. Amos took in his green Hunter wellies, waxed jacket and red-checked shirt and frowned. He looked down at the neat rows, but as far as he could see, Freya's berries were glistening little orbs of pearlescent white.

'Much like yourself, Stephen,' Freya replied. 'A little too much sauce again last night, was it? Or is your complexion always that colour?'

Stephen glared at her, his mouth trying to form the clever comeback he so desperately sought, but Freya simply smiled and took Amos' arm.

'All this talk of sauce reminds me;

time for a bacon butty, I reckon. Think I'll have an egg in mine as well. Can't beat a fried egg in the morning, can you, all oozing and dripping? Just the thing to set you up for the day. Come on, Amos, my treat.' She smiled sweetly at Stephen who had visibly paled. 'You should have one too, put a bit of colour in your cheeks.'

Freya glanced at her watch as they walked across the yard, heading incongruously for a ramshackle tin shed that looked like the last place you might get a bacon butty from. 'We don't really have time for this just yet, but anything to get away from that slimeball.'

'Would his last name be Henderson by any chance?'

'Yeah,' she replied, a harsh tone in her normally soft voice. 'I've never been able to figure out what his problem is except perhaps an extremely high opinion of himself. It's not as if their farm is any different to anyone else's, but Stephen likes to play Lord of the Manor. Everybody knows that the minute he can, he'll sell up and cash in to fund his lavish life-style. He's only interested in money.'

'He has a brother, doesn't he? I've seen him in the village a few times.'

Freya gave a small snort. 'Yeah, Sam will be around here somewhere, hiding in Stephen's shadow. You can bet your life that it was him that did all the hard work to get that lot ready for sale today, though.'

Amos squinted into the sun, a small smile tugging at the corners of his mouth. 'You don't take any prisoners, do you?'

She stopped then, turning around to face him. 'I take as I find, Amos. When my dad died, I soon found out who my real friends were, and believe me, the Hendersons were not on the list.' She glared at him, daring to be contradicted.

Amos decided that changing the subject might be the best move. 'Look if you're pushed for time, I could go and get breakfast?'

Her brown eyes softened again. 'That's a deal then,' she replied, tucking a ten-pound note into Amos' hand.

* * *

sell up and cash in to fund his lavish life-
style. He's only interested in money.

By the time Amos returned to her, Freya
had already laid out half the wreaths
into her earmarked pens, and was just
fetching another load from the van,
ingeniously threaded onto a broom pole
so that she could carry them. She was
pleased with them this year. She'd really
found her style now, and it was clear
from looking at what the other traders
had to offer, that hers were a little different. It had been hard work, though,
painstakingly collecting all the greenery to make each wreath identical, and
wiring up the fruits, acorns and walnuts
that she'd added. She could only hope
that she'd get a good price for them.

It was something her dad had encouraged her to do, even when she was small,
and he always made it her task to decorate the house for Christmas. Over
the years, she had refined her skills and
had now been bringing her home-made
decorations to the fair for the last five
years. Standing back, she checked she

had them all laid uniformly, all turned the same way, and, once satisfied, finally turned to Amos to collect her breakfast.

He waved his bap appreciatively. 'Those are beautiful, Freya,' he remarked.

'Thank you.' She blushed, jumping back as a drop of runny egg just missed her coat. She licked her roll, biting off the end of bacon which the egg had dripped from. 'I'll go and get the last of them in a minute.'

She had just taken another oozing bite when someone cannoned into the back of her, followed by an immediate gushing apology.

'Oh my God, I'm so sorry . . . Oh my God . . . Freya?'

'Merry!' shrieked Freya in return, throwing her arms around the woman as best she could, hampered both by the roll in her hand and the size of the woman's stomach. 'I didn't think you were coming this year, but look at you!'

The woman pulled a rueful face. 'I know, I'm huge, and bloody due on Christmas Day, can you believe it, of all

21

the luck.'

Freya laughed. 'I think that's the best kind of luck. You have the perfect excuse to let everyone else organise Christmas and sit around with your feet up.'

'Yeah right. Like that's really going to happen. Can you see me sitting still? Not really my style, is it? Anyway, to be fair, Tom has been brilliant. I'm only here today because I've hardly lifted a finger all weekend and am feeling guilty. We do desperately need some stock, though.'

'Well, I don't think you're going to have any trouble finding some today, it's looking like it'll be a great sale. Plenty of buyers around by the look of things, although that might not necessarily be a good thing in your case.' She paused for a moment before adding shyly, 'Are you looking for anything in particular?'

'Well, holly and mistletoe, *obviously*.' She laughed, winking at Amos. 'But Tom would like some decorative pieces for the hotel as well, so I'll drag him over in a minute. Although I have to say, if you get any better, you'll price yourself out of our market. These are looking beautiful.'

'I was wondering if they were a bit too contemporary?' said Freya, biting her lip. 'Not everyone wants something different.'

Merry studied Amos for a moment before turning back to answer. 'It's true, they don't, but I don't think you'll have any trouble selling these. Anyway, enough shop talk for now. This poor man has been standing here patiently while we gossip away.' She thrust out her hand. 'I'm Merrilees Parker, but not surprisingly everyone calls me Merry.'

Amos grasped her hand and nodded. 'I approve, and very appropriate for the time of year.'

'Sorry,' butted in Freya. 'I'm hopeless at introductions. Merry and I have known each other for a gazillion years. She's a florist by trade, although she and her husband also run a hotel in Worcester.

And Merry, this is Amos, and he . . . well, he's been helping me out a bit on the farm.'

'Still can't get Gareth interested then, Freya? Never mind, maybe he'll come round. It'll hit him one day just how boring accountancy is, and then he'll be brewing cider with the best of them.'

'Hmm, maybe,' replied Freya, sounding doubtful. 'Anyway, there might not be a one day, Merry. I've finally had to put the place on the market. This will probably be my last year.'

Her friend's face fell. 'Oh Freya, no, you can't do that. Is there really no other way? I thought when we last spoke that things were picking up a bit.'

'Not enough it would seem. Believe me, if there was another way, I'd have taken it. Gareth did all the sums, and we're just going to get deeper into debt. I only just managed to get the harvest in this year, but I want to be making cider and juices myself, Merry, not selling my apples to other people so that they can do it. The trouble is I can't afford to pay for help or new machinery, both of which I need.

'There's just me flogging myself to

death, and however hard I pretend, it's not enough. Gareth is never going to be a farmer, Merry, and it's wrong to make him try. He's been good to me, you know ... since Dad died. I have to respect that.' She blew out her cheeks. 'So ... this is it, one last push; out with a bang with any luck, and then I'll be heading for the suburbs and a two-up, two-down.'

Merry pulled Freya into another hug. 'You know we'll help if we can, don't you? I'm not sure what we can do, but we'll think of something.'

'That's very kind of you, but really, it's okay. I'll just have to get used to it. Nothing stays the same forever, Merry.'

There was real sadness in her friend's eyes as Merry pulled away. 'I must go and find Tom. I'll catch up with you later, okay?'

'Okay.'

★   ★   ★

Amos watched Freya for a moment, unsure what to say. He'd had no idea that things were quite so bad. 'Is Merry a good friend?'

Freya's grin was wide. 'The best; we grew up together. Our mums had beds next to each other in the maternity ward, and because they were always together, so were we. We don't see each other as often as we'd like to now that she's married and moved away, but we've always kept in touch. When Mum left, I practically lived at their house.'

'Her name means one who has psychic powers, did you know that?' he replied, swallowing hard. The more he got to know Freya, the more he realised what a bum deal life had dealt her. She had every reason to be bitter but was very far from it. He had a feeling that Freya's holly would always have berries on it.

'What, Merry, psychic?' She laughed. 'She didn't even realise she was pregnant for about five months! It's a nice idea, though.' She looked down at her roll, now cold and congealing in her hand. 'I don't suppose . . . ?'

Amos shook his head vehemently. 'No thanks. But I'll go and find a bin for you if you like. It looks like you have folk waiting to talk to you.' He motioned with his head and, collecting her half-eaten breakfast, wandered off. He had spied Stephen Henderson in the distance and wondered if he might be lucky enough to find a bin in his vicinity.

Things were really picking up now; the place was heaving with people amid good-natured calling and laughing, together with some more serious discussions, and if the conversations Amos had overheard were anything to go by, it looked like bidding was going to be lively. By the time he returned to Freya he could hardly see her amid the bustle that was crowding around. All eyes seemed to be on a tall man in a green coat, who carried some kind of a long stick. As Amos watched, Freya motioned him over.

'That's the auctioneer,' she said, checking her phone again. 'I think we're just about to start.'

Almost as soon as she had voiced the words, a piercing whistle rang out across the yard, and the sound fell away, leaving near silence in its wake. The sale had begun.

* * *

It was nearly seven by the time Freya walked in, the kitchen still in darkness. She dumped her bags on the table and followed the sound of the television to the living room. This too was in darkness save for the flickering glare cast by the football match that Gareth was watching. She stood for a couple of minutes in the gloom, wondering if he'd even realised she was there, before flicking on the light, making Gareth jump. He whirled around to face her.

'Christ, that's bright.'

'Sorry. Just checking you were still alive as the house is in total darkness.'

Gareth peered back at the screen.

'God, is it that late? I hadn't realised.

I only popped in here to catch the score. What a game, though.'

'Popped in with your tea and a beer.'

'Ah, well . . . yes. I wasn't sure what time you'd be back you see.'

Freya picked up his mobile phone from the coffee table beside him and pressed a button to bring the screen to life. She looked at it for a moment and then handed it silently to him, her text messages all in a row. Then she left the room.

Amos was coming in through the back door as she filled the kettle. She greeted him with a warm smile.

'What do you fancy for tea, Amos? Gareth's already eaten.'

'Um, I'm probably okay, don't worry,' he replied, flicking a glance out through the open door. 'I've put the gear back in the barn, is that okay?'

'Perfect, thank you. I could make us some beans on toast? I'm not sure I'm up for much more than that, my feet are killing me.'

Amos grinned. 'It was a brilliant day,

wasn't it? You did well I think?'

'I did fantastically! I can't believe it,' she squealed, giving a little jump of excitement. 'I just hope I can pull it off. It's a lot of work you know.'

'The best things often are, but I'm happy to help. It's very kind of you to let me stay.'

'It's purely mercenary believe me — kindness has nothing to do with it!' She laughed. 'I need your manpower.'

The kitchen doorway darkened for a second as Gareth's bulky frame passed through it.

'Let me do that, love,' he said with a pointed look at Amos. He took the kettle from Freya. 'You must be exhausted. Go and sit down for a bit, and I'll rustle up something for your tea.'

Amos looked from one to the other. 'I'll maybe go and check that the chooks have put themselves to bed, shall I?'

Freya nodded gratefully as Amos made himself scarce.

'Oh, I had the most brilliant day, Gareth,' she launched in before he could

30

start. She really wasn't in the mood for an argument tonight. 'We sold everything, and I got an incredible price for the mistletoe, but not only that, Tom placed an order with me for wreaths and decorations for the hotel. He said he was really impressed with them. Of course Merry might have had a hand in that, but I don't care, they want thirty-two of each for next Saturday; can you believe it?'

He came up behind her, sliding his arms around her waist and nuzzling the side of her neck.

'See, I told you you were amazing. That's fantastic news, Freya,' he said, dropping a soft kiss on the weak spot just behind her ear. 'Is that why he's here?'

She tried not to stiffen. 'I need help, Gareth, that's all. I met him on the road today and offered him a lift. He wasn't going in any particular direction, so I suggested he give me a hand at the fair. He was incredibly helpful today, lugging stuff around for me, and he really got the buyers going. He has nowhere to go tonight; I couldn't just leave him there.'

31

'And that's your problem because? You can't keep picking up waifs and strays just because you feel sorry for them.'

'He's not a waif and stray; he's a person, Gareth. I know you don't like him, but he's done nothing wrong, and I didn't pick him up because I feel sorry for him. He's not looking for pity if that's what you think; he's willing to work hard for his bed and board. Considering what I've got coming up this next week, I'm going to need all the help I can get.'

Gareth pulled back a little and moved his hands to cup her face. 'I don't want you to get hurt, that's all. You know nothing about this man, and yet you've invited him into our home, at a time when you're feeling very vulnerable.'

'Oh, I get it,' said Freya, pulling her head back. 'You've nothing to be jealous about you know, I've told you a hundred times. Amos is old enough to be my . . . dad,' she choked, the words sticking suddenly in her throat, and with that, she burst into tears, all the day's tension and anxiety catching up with her.

She clung to Gareth as he rubbed her back, pulling her woollen hat from her head and burying his face in her hair, which he said always smelled of apples.

'I should have made you some tea. I'm sorry, I just didn't think. Look, why don't I run you a bath, and I'll bring you a tray up to bed? You're exhausted, and a good night's sleep will do you the world of good.'

She rubbed her cheek against the softness of his sweatshirt, wanting so much to accept his platitudes and allow herself to be pacified. But there was still a spark of hurt inside her that wouldn't go away. She was tired, she was overwrought and emotional, but more than that she was excited and elated with her success today. She wanted someone to share that excitement with and help her to plan. She wanted interested questions and to share a common sense of purpose. She wanted to feel encouraged. Slowly, she disentangled herself from Gareth's arms.

'Was your phone not working today? Only I sent you quite a few messages. I

33

thought you might have wished me luck.'

Gareth squeezed her arms and turned back to the kettle on the stove as it began its whistling alert. 'Sorry love, it's a bit awkward at work. You know how it is.'

2

Amos stood and watched as the car made its way down the track, Gareth's exhaust billowing white clouds into the icy morning air. He'd spotted Freya going into the henhouse a few minutes earlier and hoped that's where he'd find her now. He felt somehow that he should apologise, although he was well aware that he hadn't actually done anything wrong.

She was talking to herself when he got there, or rather to the hens, a continual sing-song stream of chatter as one might talk to a child. He lifted the latch on the door of the coop and cleared his throat.

'Scrambled eggs on toast or an omelette?' said Freya, without turning around. Amos' mouth began to water, and his stomach gave an appreciative lurch. Staying for tea hadn't seemed such a good idea last night. 'Please tell me you didn't sleep in the barn last night?' she added.

When he didn't answer, she whirled

around to face him, three eggs in one hand and two in the other. 'Right, come with me,' she said.

Amos followed her meekly back into the kitchen, which, after the air outside, felt rather like a sauna, but right now, the most comforting place on earth. Freya set the eggs down on the table, holding her hand over them just for a second to be sure they didn't roll. 'Sit down a minute.' Amos did as he was told.

A few minutes later, she placed a huge mug of tea and a plate of toast swimming in butter in front of him. She motioned for Amos to start eating. 'Right, while you're tucking into that lot, let's get a couple of things straight, shall we? Firstly, can I just say that I'm sorry that Gareth is being such a prat.'

Amos looked up sharply at her words, but she held her hand up to finish. 'This is my house, and who I invite into it is my business. I know Gareth is my boyfriend, and perhaps I sound a bit disloyal, but he's got no right to moan about you being around, especially when he's so completely uninterested in everything I'm trying to do here. We've got a busy week ahead, and I haven't got time to pander to his selfish and childish arguments.' She stared at Amos to check whether he was still following her. 'Secondly, you have a room in the house and a bathroom which you are very welcome to use, so please Amos, don't sleep in the barn; it's bloody freezing out there.'

Amos took a slug of tea and hacked off the corner of a piece of toast. 'Rant over?' He smiled.

'Rant over.' Freya smiled back. 'I'm glad we understand one another.'

'It strikes me that what we need is a plan of action,' added Amos. 'It's not just the wreaths that need to be made, is it? You'll need more holly and mistletoe for next week's fair, and that doesn't include all your normal jobs. Let me finish this, and we'll make a list.'

'I tell you what, I've got an even better idea. There's plenty of hot water left, so why don't you go and grab a shower and warm yourself up a bit while I make us a proper breakfast; then we'll see where we go from there.'

Amos touched his hand to her sleeve. 'Thank you.'

* * *

It was noon before they stopped again for a welcome cuppa. They had spent the morning walking the fields and deciding what to cut and when. Freya would need a good deal of greenery for her arrangements, but there were still two mistletoe sales left, and of course she would need a little left over to decorate the farmhouse too. She never tired of the orchards. Whatever the weather, whatever the time of year, there was always some new wonder to catch her eye; baby rabbits running and chasing across the fields, frothy clouds of elderflower blossom in the hedgerow, or row after row of apple blossom, its pale beauty against a blue summer sky a sight she would never forget. Even on the darker days she loved it; those still October mornings when the sky hardly seemed to clear the ground, but where, here in the orchard, the sparkle of dew on cobwebs really was like diamonds, and the air was heavy with the scent of apples.

She had never known anywhere else, and the thought that she might soon have to leave was almost unbearable. She'd taken it all for granted. She hadn't realised until her dad died how much he had protected her from, how much of a struggle it must have been for him to keep things going and how much he had sacrificed over the years. She hadn't realised either quite how much debt they were in, and she felt enormously guilty that she'd never known. Her dad had carried that burden solely on his shoulders, and although she knew he wouldn't have had it any other way, she couldn't help wondering whether it had contributed to his early death; he had, after all, been only sixty-three.

Her mobile had flashed during the morning with a missed call from a number that she had been expecting. She couldn't go on deliberately avoiding these calls and finally decided to voice the nagging thoughts that had been plaguing her.

'Do you think I'm mad, Amos?'

'Possibly,' he replied ambiguously. 'But there's several definitions of mad in my book, not all of them bad I might add, so which variant do you think you might be?'

'Well, all this; doing all these orders, going to sales — for what? The estate agent rang this morning, and I know it's because he's got someone he wants to show around. Sure, I'll make a bit of money from the sales, but it's never going to be enough to save this place, so why am I doing it, why am I putting myself through this?'

Amos took in a long slow breath, considering the question, and then gently let it out again. 'That's not something I can answer, Freya. Only you know why.'

Freya screwed up her face. 'Well, that's no bloody good,' she wheedled. 'Can't you make something up, to make me feel better? Or even not to make me feel better, but to make me see sense instead?'

'Possibly. But I don't know you all that well.'

'You know me well enough. Anyway, you have that wise man thing about you, like you've got everyone sussed. So, tell me why you think I'm doing this.'

'Are you sure you really want me to tell you?'

'Yes, for God's sake,' she groaned. 'Put me out of my misery.'

Amos regarded her for a moment, and then he looked around the room she loved so much, with its warm colours and comfortable furnishings.

'I think it's because there's so much of you in this house, Freya, that you're scared you won't exist outside of it,' he said slowly. 'You've lived here your whole life, and when your mum left, it was just you and your dad against the world, and this place, well, it became your fortress if you like. Now that he's gone, it's the only thing that ties you to him, and now that the house is threatened as well, it's like you're threatened too, like you don't know who you are, or more importantly who you want to be. It's time to find out, Freya, that's all. There's no madness involved. I think if I'd had this life, this house, I'd do everything I could to keep it too. But if it really has to go, then see it as your opportunity to find out what's important to you; and when you do find out, don't let go of it. You never know, things might surprise you.'

'What if I don't know what I want,' she whispered, her gaze still locked on his.

'You will, Freya, you will. Now make the call.'

★ ★ ★

The agent was prompt, more's the pity. Stephen Henderson came in first, his arrogant manner slightly subdued by the colourful black eye he was wearing, but that didn't stop him from gazing around the kitchen with a very annoying grin on his face. Freya shook his hand, desperate to ask about the eye, but promising herself that at least one of them should show some manners.

The agent was the same one who had come to value the property and draw up the details. She'd gone to school with him, which was a little embarrassing, but then that happened a lot around here. He took Freya to one side almost as soon as he entered the room.

'I know you'll be expecting to show them around, Freya, but can I make a suggestion? Actually, it wasn't mine, it was Sam's, but, on this occasion, I happen to agree. Usually, I'm very happy for the vendor to chat to prospective buyers; it can lend a more relaxed air to proceedings and is often helpful when questions are asked. But since both brothers know the property well, it would seem a bit superfluous, and I wondered whether you might find it difficult, well, awkward, you know. Sam thought this way might be easier for you.' He gave a nervous smile, half expecting to be shot down in flames.

Freya hadn't considered this, but it

was a kind thought. She looked at Amos for guidance, who gave a small nod. She was blushing and she knew it, sitting down at the table quickly to hide her colour. For some reason, an old and deeply inappropriate memory had just popped into her head, of her and Sam, from a time when they had been very good friends. But why today of all days when she hadn't thought about him that way in years? It was a good thing that she and Amos were to remain sitting at the table because, right now, Freya really didn't think she'd have anything coherent to say. The moment soon passed, however, as Stephen's voice floated up from the passageway. Ignorant moron, of course it looked like an old-fashioned pantry; that's exactly what it was.

Amos kept up a low babble of conversation the whole time, and she knew it was to prevent her from hearing further snippets of conversation. She was thinking about what he had said, though, and how accurate his assessment of her had been. She shouldn't really be surprised.

The more she got to know Amos, the more fascinating she found him, but she hadn't realised she had been wearing her heart on her sleeve quite as obviously as she had. Their discussion had focused her mind, and as much as she hadn't wanted to make the decisions that were facing her, they were long overdue, and all the months she had spent deliberating her various options hadn't brought her any further forward. For some reason, that had changed today, and she knew that she could no longer hide from what was surely the inevitable. It would take a miracle to save Appleyard, but if she had to go, she had to go, and now she must fight for a future beyond this house.

Something cut across her thoughts, and she suddenly became aware of what Amos was saying.

'You never mentioned that before.' Freya laughed. 'That's priceless.'

'Well, I can imagine Stephen Henderson gets himself into all sorts of scrapes from what I've been hearing, and I don't suppose it's the first time he's had a black eye. I might have expected him to get belted by some chap who bore him a grudge, but I never thought it would be his brother.'

'And this happened at the fair? Oh, I wish I'd seen it. Good for Sam. I wonder what they were arguing about, though.'

'I was too far away to hear what was actually being said, but whatever it was, Sam didn't like it. I could see they were arguing, and then Sam turned as if to leave but instead swung round with an almighty punch. He had Stephen on the floor.'

'No wonder he looked a little sheepish when he first came in. Oh, Amos, you've made my day.'

'Ssh, they're coming back; straight faces back on, no laughing,' said Amos sternly.

Freya tried to stifle her giggles. She thought of Stephen poking his nose into all her things, and that did the trick, but then reminded herself that it was a necessary evil. She knew she was biased, but Appleyard was a handsome house;

not huge, but a good size nonetheless, of warm red brick and with a pleasing symmetry. It was hard to think about it objectively, but its welcoming rooms were just what people wanted, according to the estate agent.

By the time they'd all arrived back in the kitchen, Freya even managed a welcoming smile. She got up to show them out as they all did the thank-you-for-showing-us-round, we'll-be-in-touch routine. Freya didn't doubt that they would; in a way it hardly mattered what the house was like, Stephen Henderson had been trying to get his hands on their farm for years.

Later that night as Freya lay next to Gareth listening to his rhythmic snoring, she found herself thinking about Sam for some unaccountable reason.

★　★　★

Four doors down at the other end of the house, Amos lay on the floor, as was his custom, gazing at the stars through the window. He was also thinking about

Sam, but for an entirely different reason. When they'd met earlier, his attention had been consumed by the young man. He'd only ever seen Sam from a distance, but up close, he'd been able to see the family resemblance. He had Stephen's features, but more refined so, instead of looking squashed and pudgy, he was a very attractive man. And while he had none of his brother's stature, his clothes suited him too; he seemed relaxed in them whereas his brother always looked like he was dressing up. He rubbed the back of his neck thoughtfully, another piece of his jigsaw falling into place.

3

The call from the estate agent didn't come until Friday afternoon, much as Freya had expected. It was all part of the game, and it certainly wouldn't do for the Hendersons to appear too keen; although Freya imagined that Stephen had found the two-day interval rather trying. Despite his disparaging remarks about her house, she knew it had been on his hit list for years. He'd even had the gall to ask her not long after her dad's funeral when she was putting it on the market. The fact that it had only taken eight months before she'd been forced to, stuck in her craw, but she reminded herself that it was a means to an end.

She actually laughed out loud when she heard what they were prepared to offer. She had expected it to be low, but fifty thousand pounds below the asking price was plain ridiculous. Having reminded the estate agent that they had deliberately priced the property compet-itively to take into account the time of year, she left him in no doubt that his client either needed to be sensible or quite frankly piss off.

'Do you think they'll come up?' asked Amos as she returned to the table.

Freya picked up another length of rib-bon and proceeded to twist it expertly into a bow. 'I think so, although you can never really tell with Stephen. He's that arrogant he seems to think his money is worth more than anyone else's.' She swapped hands, winding wire around the bow to secure it and adding a tail which would fasten it to the wreath. 'Much might also depend of course on how much influence Sam has. You see the thing with Stephen is that he convinces himself he wants something really badly, but then when he gets it, he can't be bothered. He doesn't put the effort into their own farm; it's all down to Sam. Ste-phen just likes the title of landowner and the ability it gives him to swank about. He's always been the same, ever since he was little.'

'So what's the story with the two brothers then?'

Freya paused for a moment, raising her eyebrows in query. 'What do you mean?'

'Well, I might be mistaken,' ventured Amos, 'but you seem to be rather fonder of one than the other. I wondered if there was any reason for that.'

'Oh there are lots of reasons for that, but none that I'm prepared to go into just now.'

'Fair enough.' Amos shrugged with a smile. 'It was worth a try.'

Freya smiled too. 'Another time perhaps. Now how many of these blessed things have I got left to do?'

Amos counted up. 'Thirty-seven,' he said with a grimace. 'Would another cup of tea help? I'm not sure what else I can do.'

'Tea would be lovely, and you could always peel the veg for tea if you wanted a job. I'm just going to make a chuck-it-all-in vegetable soup, which requires very little effort on my part, but fortunately tastes like I've been slaving over a hot stove all day.'

'So what's the grand plan now?'

'There's nothing terribly grand about it,' started Freya, scratching her nose. 'I do need to sell the house, and pretty quickly too, but after that I have a few options. I had another chat with Merry on the phone this morning, and there are a few ideas I'm exploring with her.' She looked down at the table. 'I love doing all this — making things, the decorations, everything really. I think there's a market for this type of thing, but I need a base to do it from, and once the house has gone, that's what I don't have.'

'Is there no one else interested in this place?'

'Nope. Dead as a dodo. I shouldn't have left it as late as I did putting it on the market, but there you go, one to chalk up to experience.'

'Understandable, in the circumstances.'

Freya tilted her head to one side. 'Perhaps. Not everyone sees it that way.' She laid another wired ribbon on the table. 'Right, I'd better get these finished. It doesn't take long to fix them to the wreaths, but I'd rather get them all finished today. That way I can get them over to Tom and Merry first thing in the morning.'

★ ★ ★

'Well, this is cosy.'

Freya looked up at the sound of the voice by the door and tutted audibly. 'Don't be such a prat, Gareth. I'm sitting here finishing Tom's decorations off for tomorrow, and Amos is reading. We're not having wild abandoned sex on the rug in front of the fire.' She looked pointedly at the wall on the clock. 'Nice of you to let me know you were going to be late.'

'It's Friday, I always go down the pub after work on a Friday.' He pouted.

'Yes, and you usually let me know. I made soup for tea, which is now stone cold, but there's still some in the pan if you want to heat it up.'

Gareth had the grace to look a little ashamed at this. 'Oh. Er, well, I ate at the pub, sorry.'

'My point exactly, so please don't come in here throwing wild accusations around.' She glared at Gareth.

'Anyway, I've got some news if you're interested,' added Gareth, still a little sulky, but with the beginnings of a triumphant gleam in his eyes. 'I didn't exactly waste my time while I was down the pub.'

'I'll pour some tea,' said Freya, lifting the teapot from the middle of the table. 'Sit down.'

Gareth dumped his work bag on a chair and rummaged around in its depths.

'Well, for starters, I got these at lunchtime. Two of them have just been reduced and are real bargains.' He placed a sheaf of papers on the table and pushed them towards Freya who eyed them warily. When she made no move to pick them up, Gareth rifled through them impatiently. 'This one in particular is a real gem. Very clean and well cared for, but it's been on the market for a while and the owners have already found a place so are desperate to sell.'

Eventually, Freya picked up the property details and scanned through them, returning to the one that Gareth had pointed out and studying it more carefully.

'But these are all on estates.'

'I know, they're brilliant. Full of people the same age as us, with schools and shops nearby, and this one is just around the corner from work. It's on that new estate just up past the business park.'

'The gardens look very small.'

'But you wouldn't want a big garden, would you? Not after this place. And just think, we could move in the New Year; fresh start and all that.'

Freya sighed. 'But that's all supposing I can sell this place. That might take a little time.'

Gareth sat back in his chair with a triumphant grin. 'Ah, but you see that's the best bit. I got talking to Stephen Henderson in the pub tonight. I did a cracking deal with him. Who needs bloody estate agents, eh?'

'Go on,' said Freya in a low tone, her spine stiffening.

'We got chatting, and he mentioned he'd put in an offer on the place — '

'Yeah, I bet he did.'

'Look, are you going to let me tell you or what! I felt a bit of a tit, to be honest, seeing as I didn't even know he'd been to see the place, or put in an offer.'

Freya remained silent.

'Anyway, never mind that now. He's really keen to get this deal under wraps, so we had a bit of a chat. I know you turned his offer down flat, and he doesn't blame you for that, but all he needed was a bit of buttering up. Honestly, Freya, I would have thought you'd realise that. I bought him a few drinks and we chatted a bit more and . . . what do you think of this . . . he's agreed to come up another ten grand on his offer, and...' he paused here for effect, leaning in towards Freya with a grin, 'provided we can get the sale though quick, he'll give us twenty-five thousand in cash on the side.'

'No,' said Freya flatly.

Gareth's mouth hung open for a moment. 'What do you mean, no? It's a bloody good deal, only fifteen grand lower than the asking price. We'll have a wodge of cash in the bank to spend as we like and can buy a house outright with no mortgage. Think of how much money we'll have every month not having to fork out on the enormous bills we have here.'

'I said no, Gareth.'

'Oh, for God's sake,' he hissed. 'Will you get over yourself with that bloody man? I've got us a brilliant deal, and you're being stubborn because you don't like him. His money's as good as anyone else's, Freya, and you're not going to get another deal.'

Freya's nostrils flared. 'Firstly, you don't know I'm not going to get another deal, and secondly what I do about this place is very much my decision, seeing as this is my house.'

'Oh well, thanks a bunch, that's bloody

gratitude for you. I'm trying to do the best for us, and you throw it straight back in my face. At least I'm trying to do something constructive, not wallowing in self-pity about this stupid house, which, I might add is a noose around our necks.'

Freya risked a glance at Amos, knowing how awkward this must be for him. 'It's a noose around *my* neck, Gareth, not yours. And while we're on the subject, let's just look at everything you're doing for *us*. Let's look at the hours you've put into this place, helping me to keep it going. Let's look at the help you've given me with the harvest, or selling my fruit, or even just getting the mistletoe ready for the sales. A big fat zero, Gareth, that's what. I might not be able to stay in this house, but all I was asking for was a bit of support and understanding of how I feel, instead of trying to ship me out to some soulless brick box. This perfect vision you have for our future, Gareth, is all about you; it's your dream, and you've never considered for one moment how I feel, or what I want.'

'But I'm doing this for you, you stupid cow. I'm trying to save you from yourself if you'd only stop and listen. You're so bloody blinkered about this place, you won't think beyond the end of your nose. I haven't put the hours in on this place, as you so charmingly put it, because I can see it would be flogging a dead horse and only encourage you. I want a future for us, Freya, but you're frittering away everything we have, and if you carry on, we'll lose the best opportunity we've ever had too.'

Freya's hands were clenching and unclenching in her lap. 'The best opportunity *you've* ever had you mean. You've never contributed financially to this place, but you'd be very happy for me to sell up and feather your nest with a nice little mortgage-free house. Well played, Gareth, well played.'

Gareth snatched back the estate agent's brochures from the table. 'So is that what it all comes down to in the end, Freya, your money? In my book that's not what a true partnership is all about.' He lurched up from the table, his face beetroot. 'Keep your bloody money. I hope you'll be very happy.'

'I will, because it's not as if you've earned any of it. How soon was it after Dad died that you moved in here, eh? It used to be a partnership, Gareth, but it hasn't been one for a long time; just up to the point where you thought your grand prize was within reach, in fact. I cook, clean, clear up after you, wash your clothes and generally run around after you each and every day as well as everything else I have to do here, while you go out to work. Not that I see any of the fruits of your labour. What exactly do you contribute to this so-called partnership?'

'I've been saving my money for us, putting it aside for our new life actually, if you'd bothered to ask.'

'So how much have you saved then, Mr Accountant? You've had your hands on my books these last few months, but how much have you saved for our future after you've bought that swanky new car, and had your weekends away with the boys? Not to mention that bloody cruise that was a monumental waste of money?' Freya lurched to her feet too, keeping one hand on the table.

Gareth glared at her as she held his gaze. 'Jesus, what are you accusing me of now? I don't have to stand here and listen to this.'

'How much, Gareth?'

He threw the papers onto the floor and gave the chair back an almighty shove before stalking from the room.

'Yeah right . . . I thought as much,' muttered Freya sadly.

She looked at Amos for a moment who was still pinned to his chair unable to move, and then slowly sat back down, her body deflating like a balloon. She rested her head on the table. 'Oh, dear Lord,' she said to no one in particular.

4

Amos certainly hadn't slept much, and he reckoned Freya had slept even less, but somehow, he missed her the next morning. She must have gone out at the crack of dawn. The house was still in darkness as he crept downstairs, checking as he did so that Gareth's car was still in the yard. He didn't suppose that he'd be up too early, but one thing was for certain, Amos didn't want to be anywhere near him when he did.

Taking an apple from the fruit bowl and a hunk of the fresh bread he had made the day before, he slipped on his jacket and boots and softly closed the kitchen door behind him. He didn't know how far it was to the Hendersons' farm, but he knew the general direction it lay in and he'd enjoy the walk at any rate. There was no doubt in his mind that Sam Henderson would be the only one up at this hour of the morning, and there were a couple of things that Amos wanted to chat to him about. He wasn't quite sure why Stephen was so keen to buy Appleyard in such a hurry, but something about the whole thing didn't smell right to him.

He'd only gone a matter of a mile or so when he felt a familiar prickle on the back of his neck. He walked on a little further, the feeling growing stronger with each step until he had to stop by the side of the road and wait for the feeling to pass. If he concentrated hard, he could usually sort out the 'noise' in his head until he understood its sound, but this time, nothing he did could alleviate it. He leaned on the farm gate for a few more moments feeling slightly nauseous when a movement in the field caught his eye, and suddenly he understood. In the distance a rider was putting a horse through its paces and, without a second thought, Amos braced his arms on the top of the gate and swung himself over.

The field was large, and it took him some while to reach them, the horse becoming aware of him first, slowing from a canter to a walk, and finally stopping altogether despite the best efforts of its rider. Amos could sense the confusion in the young man as his horse steadfastly refused to move until, finally, Amos was close enough for him to register his presence. The rider raised a hand, in warning, not in greeting, but Amos paid him no heed. The huge bay stallion walked over to him, eventually standing quietly by his side.

The rider shielded his eyes from the low morning sun as he squinted to get a better view.

'By rights, you should be dead by now, coming up on a horse like that.'

Amos stroked the bay's nose while it blew steamy breaths into his hand.

'You're Sam, aren't you?' he asked. 'Sam Henderson? Sorry, we weren't properly introduced the other day.'

The rider nodded, peering closer until a gleam of recognition appeared in his eyes. He slipped his feet out of the stirrups and slid down from the horse, rubbing its flank for a moment before turning back to Amos.

'You're the chap who's been helping Freya, aren't you? You were with her at the mistletoe sales as well. I'm sorry, I don't know your name.'

'It's Amos. Amos Fry.'

Sam shook his hand. 'Well, Amos, you either know a lot about horses or you're a bloody idiot. Bailey here doesn't normally take too kindly to strangers.'

'I'm sorry I alarmed you, but Bailey and I seem to be getting along just fine,' Amos replied as the horse nuzzled his hand. 'I was on my way to see you actually, Freya mentioned you.'

Sam grimaced. 'Well, I can imagine what she had to say, and none of it complimentary I'm sure.'

'Actually, it's only your brother she dislikes.'

He laughed. 'Really . . . ? Oh, well yes, he does seem to have that effect on people. Anyway, what can I do for you, Amos?'

'Have you spoken to your brother since last night?'

'You must be joking, it's only eight o'clock. My brother won't be up for hours yet.'

'Well, in that case, perhaps we could walk a little, and I'll explain.'

* * *

Amos eventually found Freya sitting in the dark on a gate at the far end of the orchard. He'd also found only one car in the yard upon his return, and the scribbled note from Gareth on the side in the kitchen. She'd been crying of course.

He peeled her icy hands away from the cold metal of the gate and led her unyielding into the house where the fire he had laid earlier was roaring. He placed a blanket around her shoulders and a mug of hot chocolate in front of her and then went to sit in one of the armchairs opposite her, where he pretended to read for half an hour before she spoke.

'I don't know why I'm upset really.'

Amos looked up at her. 'It's human

nature to mourn something when it's gone.'

She ran a hand wearily through her hair. 'It was stupid, arguing like that. I was tired, and he was drunk, it wasn't the best time to have a discussion.'

'No, perhaps it wasn't. But given a better time, would the words have been any different?'

'No,' she said slowly. 'I don't think they would.' She let out a long sigh. 'I think I've probably been feeling that way for quite a while, I just didn't realise it until I opened my mouth.'

'How long had you been together?'

'Nearly four years. Too long probably. I harboured dreams once that he would ask me to marry him, and we could run this place together, but he never did, and as time went on, it became obvious that he was never really interested. We don't have all that much in common. I mean, he doesn't even much like being outside. A long walk in the country is his idea of hell, but we've always got on quite well, and he was very good to me when Dad died.' She looked down at her mug of chocolate, swilling it gently. 'I wanted someone to share in what we had here, but that person was never going to be Gareth, I can see that now. I've let him down too. He thought I wanted the same things he did, but, in truth, I couldn't live the kind of life he wanted either, a little piece of me would have died each day until we ended up hating each other.'

'Then you've made the right decision. Our choices in life aren't always easy, but if they come from the heart, they're usually the right ones, I've found. Feeling sad for what has passed is normal, but it also frees you to face the future without the weight of hurt and disappointment. These things are often barriers to what lies beyond, and now, without them, you can be open to possibility once more.'

'But what am I going to do, Amos? It's nearly Christmas, and I've probably totally blown it with the Hendersons. I don't want to bow down to Stephen, but I really could do with the money, especially after today.' She took another sip of her chocolate, staring morosely into her mug.

'But I didn't think Gareth contributed financially from what you said. How will his leaving make things any worse for you?'

'It won't, but that's not what I meant. I had a phone call from Merry today. She's had an idea that might give me a way out of all this; without the cash, though, I might not be able to make it happen.'

'That sounds like it could be good news?'

'It is, yes. They've given me a repeat order for the hotel for the next four weeks, right up until Christmas. With that and what I make from the mistletoe sales, it will keep me going through to January, but I will need to find something then, which is where Merry's idea comes in.'

Amos got up to throw another log on the fire. 'Go on,' he said, poking at the embers.

'Well, it seems like they've decided that trying to run two businesses might not be so easy with a small child; at some point they're going to sell the florist shop. They've got someone in there at the moment covering for Merry, but she wants to finish at the end of January anyway. To cut a long story short, Merry has offered it to me to run for a few months while she's busy with the baby with a view to buying it if I find it suits me. Well, obviously, I can't be in two places at once, so I really need to be out of here early in the New Year. Tom has offered me a room at their hotel until I can find somewhere to live.'

'So it sounds as if you have a plan?'

'I might have. But like I said I really need to get this place sold. It's very good of Merry to offer the shop to me, but I can't keep them hanging on, they need to make plans too. The extra orders are good news, but they'll take up a lot of my time as well, and I don't see how I can possibly get everything done.' She rubbed her eyes, which still looked red from her crying.

'Seems to me as if you have no option really. You'll have to speak to the Hendersons and see what happens; just take one thing at a time. As it happens, I bumped into Sam this morning while I was out walking.'

Freya sat up a little straighter. 'You bumped into him?'

'Well, not exactly, he was out riding, but our paths crossed. We got talking, and I happened to mention the deal that Gareth is supposed to have done with his brother. Not surprisingly, given the early hour, he hadn't yet spoken to Stephen and knew nothing about it, but I'd say he was pretty curious. Perhaps you ought to have a chat with him.'

Freya narrowed her eyes. 'Just how exactly do you bump into someone on a horse, Amos? What are you up to?'

'Not a thing,' he replied blithely. 'But it did occur to me that it wouldn't hurt to keep a closer eye on them than usual, just to check that things go according to plan. As it happens, what with Stephen being such a monumental waste of space, Sam is feeling a little busy right now and since the young lad who's been helping him out has come down with glandular fever, when I mentioned that I might have a few hours spare if he needed any help, he rather bit my hand off.'

'Amos,' said Freya in a warning tone. 'That's downright meddling.'

Amos said nothing, but stared into the fire, a small smile playing around his lips.

5

Freya really wasn't looking forward to this meeting. It was the first time she and Sam had been alone together in the same room since . . . well, for a very long time, and in the few days since Gareth had gone she'd realised how much she missed having him around. She hadn't thought they'd talked all that much, but even 'Pass the butter please' was better than no one to talk to at all.

Her dad had always told her how expressive her eyes were; big dark brown pools of her very soul, he teased her, whenever she had been trying to keep something from him. One look and any-one would guess what she was feeling, and now she was rather afraid that she was wearing an I'm-very-vulnerable, please-come-and-rescue-me air which was not the impression she wanted to give Sam at all. She was staring in the mirror again, despite having given herself a stern talking to. She had washed her hair, but that was all. Her face was resolutely devoid of make-up, and her curves were just . . . well, just plain curvy.

She had wondered if Sam would come on his own, or whether Stephen would muscle in, unable to bear anyone other than him getting the better of Freya Sherbourne. But as it happened when she opened the door, only Sam was standing there, looking very cold and, she was relieved to see, rather nervous.

She made them tea, not because she wanted any, but because it gave her something to do with her hands which suddenly didn't know how to behave. She stumbled for a moment over asking Sam whether he took sugar. Giving it to him without would seem rather knowing and presumptuous, and she wasn't sure she'd be able to look him in the eye. Better to pretend he was a stranger and ask what he preferred, as long as he didn't make some cute reference to it himself. Good grief, since when had making a cup of tea become so difficult? Fortunately,

Sam was the model guest, and they managed to end up with a cup of tea each without incident.

His attempt at conversation, though, was rather less successful as he complimented her on the homely quality of her kitchen. Normally, a safe conversational bet designed to put the hostess at ease, but under the circumstances, probably the worst thing he could have said. Of course he then realised and didn't know what to say. Freya flushed bright red and decided that a more forthright discussion was the only way forward.

'Look, Sam, I'm sorry, but to be blunt I want to sell Appleyard, you want to buy it, so let's just discuss the price and then we can hand everything over to the agent and solicitors.'

'Erm, yes, good idea,' said Sam, nodding his head vigorously. 'Right, well, I've had a chat to Stephen, and as expected his memory of the offer he made to Gareth is a little sketchy, but the essence of it was that you would end up with an amount about fifteen thousand pounds lower than the asking price. I'm not sure how you feel about this whole cash business, but it doesn't sit right with me, so I've persuaded Stephen to bin that idea if that's okay?'

Freya nodded rapidly.

'Now the bit you're not going to like is that Stephen has, as usual, been shouting his mouth off to all his cronies and he's found a chap who wants to rent this place. After all, we won't need to live in it, but this mate is going through a messy divorce and needs to move in pretty sharpish. On that basis, Stephen's agreed it would be only reasonable to offer you the full asking price provided that the sale can complete on the 10th of January. That's possible apparently as neither of us has any other properties involved. We don't need a survey, and there shouldn't be any issue over boundaries, etc. You might remember our parents had them checked a few years ago when my dad bought the strip along your bottom field.'

'Still, that seems awfully fast. I'm not

quite sure I understand Stephen's massive rush, especially at this time of year.'

Sam sighed. 'I imagine it has something to do with getting a mate out of a fix. You know how Stephen likes people owing him favours because he very often has to call them in. If I'm honest, there will probably be some sort of cash inducement involved as well, but I wouldn't worry about that. If it suits you, Freya, it's still a very good offer.'

Freya bit her lip, knowing the truth in his words. It would give her exactly what she wanted . . . and exactly what she didn't want. She'd give anything to be able to stay at Appleyard, but as it was clear she couldn't do that, then she must accept that fate was sending her somewhere else. The plans she'd made seemed good ones, and she'd be foolish to miss the only opportunity she currently had.

She nodded her head slowly. 'I know Sam, and thank you. Submit your offer through the agent, and I'll speak to my solicitor later today.' She offered her hand in the traditional manner.

Sam gazed at it sadly before taking it in his own, the warmth of it sending her somewhere she really didn't want to go. He rose to leave.

'Before you go, Sam,' said Freya, also standing up. 'Just answer me a question, will you . . . ? This all seems a bit Stephen this and Stephen that; what's in it for you, besides a load more work?'

It was a grimace really, more than a smile. 'I keep a roof over my head, Freya. And I get to stay doing what I love. Simple as that.'

She nodded and walked him to the door, frowning gently at his answer that wasn't really an answer. 'Will I see you at the sales?'

'Yes. We'll be there next week. I'll see you then.' He walked a few steps down the path before turning back. 'I'll miss you, Freya.'

Freya managed a tight smile before closing the door. She walked back into the kitchen, took down a letter she had tucked into the plate rack, and read it one more time, tears pouring down her face.

'I'm so sorry, Dad,' she whispered.

6

Freya fished about in her handbag for some painkillers. Unusually for her, she had the beginnings of a headache, and today the noise was really beginning to get to her. It was the second week in December, and the last sale was always the busiest as the selling season reached its peak, and she could hardly move for people. On the one hand, this was great for business, but she was so tired, she wished she could enjoy it more; the atmosphere was brilliant today. It would also be her last ever sale, and she wanted to savour every little drop, remember every tiny detail to store up for the future. The last thing she needed was to feel unwell.

She found a couple of tablets, and stuffed them in her mouth, swigging them down with the dregs of a cold cup of tea. She watched as a trio of Santa Clauses made its way across the yard and smiled in spite of herself. Even at the ripe old age of 35, she still felt that special kind of excitement that only came at Christmas. She sought out Amos in the crowd, trying to weave his way back to her, carrying his precious breakfast cargo.

She didn't know what she would have done without him these last couple of weeks. If she thought she'd been busy before, that was nothing compared to now, having added packing into the mix as well. Appleyard wasn't a huge house, but it was big enough, and with just her and her dad living there, they had filled every corner of available space. Freya had never had any need to declutter before, and now she was having to sort through over thirty years of memories and the stuff of life. For the moment, everything would have to go into storage, and so the less there was, the better. Given her current state of mind, however, it wasn't a task that she was finding at all easy, and were it not for Amos, she would have given up long before now. He knew when to buoy her up, when to give her space and when to just plain nag. He had been a real lifesaver.

A loud shout in her ear brought her back to the present. The sale would be starting any minute now, the hubbub reaching a crescendo as people shouted their last-minute questions and instructions. Her wreaths were all laid out in the traditional pens, but she'd been hoping to get a look at what the other sellers had to offer too. She beckoned Amos over to give her a hand up onto one of the wide metal railings that bisected a pair of pens. The auctioneers usually stood on these, so that they could see who was bidding, but Freya would only be a minute; she could be up and back down again before the sale started. She walked its length, trying to gauge the other lots and what the likely prices would be. Bidding was expected to be lively today, and she hoped that her offerings would be sufficiently distinctive to command a slightly higher price again. She could see the auctioneer coming to the end of the railings where she was standing and turned to walk back the way she had come.

As soon as she put her foot down, she knew it wouldn't end well. Her scarf had slipped off her shoulder, and she'd trapped the end of it under her boot, throwing her balance off to one side. Instinctively, she tried to throw her body backwards to compensate, but she couldn't move, her upper body pinned by the scarf around her neck. She heard Amos's warning shout but, by then, she had too much forward momentum to right herself. In the instant before the sickening crack, it flashed through her mind that putting out her hands to save her fall was a really bad idea; but by then, she had already landed, her body concertinaed on top of the arm that had crumpled beneath her.

It didn't hurt at first as she became aware of the general commotion around her, but as she tried to sit up, a searing pain ricocheted through her arm, followed swiftly by a violent wave of nausea, and her half-digested breakfast splattered onto the pair of boots in front of her.

She was aware of a soft voice talking to her, but everything else was swimming around most alarmingly and for a moment all she could do was concentrate on breathing in and out.

After a few minutes, the pain had receded to an angry buzz, and she raised her head. She was met by a pair of green eyes, which immediately elicited another groan. Of all the people at the fair today, why in God's name did it have to be Sam Henderson's boots that she'd thrown up all over? He was talking to her, and she tried to focus on what he was saying.

'Where does it hurt, Freya, just your arm?'

She'd always liked his voice. With a supreme effort, she thought about the question. Her knee was stinging, but apart from that all the pain was concentrated in her arm.

She managed a nod. 'I think so,' she whispered. 'Can I sit up?' She was aware of another person by her side and instinctively knew it was Amos.

Gradually, she realised that a space was opening up around her, and she felt a blanket settle over her. It was bright red with white reindeer on it.

'I've called an ambulance, Freya, just lie still,' said Sam.

'What? I can't go to the hospital, what about the sale . . . ? Help me to stand up, I'll be all right in a minute.'

'I bloody well will not, Freya Sherbourne, you're going to do as you're told.'

Tears sprang to Freya's eyes. 'No, you don't understand, Sam, I need to carry on. I need to sell my stuff today . . . Oh God, I've stopped the sale, haven't I? Are people really cross?'

Sam smiled. 'No one's cross, just concerned. Once we've got you sorted, they'll carry on, don't worry.'

Freya looked up at his face which was alarmingly close to hers. He hadn't shaved for a couple of days and the stubble suited him.

'Perhaps Amos could handle the sale on your behalf, Freya,' added Sam, 'if that's okay? I'm sure he's more than capable.'

Amos grinned. 'It would be a pleasure, Freya, and don't worry, I'll kick up a storm for you. Just relax, and as Sam said, do as you're told. You're in good hands. I'll see you later, okay?'

Sam flashed him a grateful look and tucked the blanket around Freya a little more.

'I can't believe I threw up on your boots,' she said.

'I know, it's not my week, is it? My horse shat on them yesterday too.'

* * *

Two and a half hours later, Freya was propped up in bed eating a piece of toast and jam which was, quite possibly, the best meal she'd ever had. A very lovely young doctor had given her a very lovely injection of something equally lovely, and now everything was ... well just lovely really; even Sam.

'Do you remember the time at the

Harvest Festival dance when I threw a glass of wine at you?' She grinned. 'All over your beautiful pristine shirt. You didn't speak to me for days.'

'Well, that's because I thought you did it on purpose. I hadn't realised you'd tripped over Mrs Courtney-Smyth's enormous feet.'

'And I was doing my best to act all sophisticated, like I drank red wine all the time, when in truth I couldn't stand the stuff and was quite happy to have got rid of it.'

'I remember your dress,' said Sam quietly. 'Deep claret-red velvet.'

Freya remembered her dress too, and she remembered the way Sam had looked at her that night. She looked at him now, on the outside, not that much different; still the same unusual green eyes, darkest brown hair that, although cut short, still liked to curl if it could, and the wide generous mouth that curved into a cheeky grin. On the inside, however, she doubted things could ever be the same, and she pulled her gaze away before she could dwell on it any longer.

'Well, I was thin then, of course, back when we were all bright young things and could wear a bin liner and still look good,' she said, trying to lighten the conversation.

'I never looked good in a bin liner.'

'Well, there were some exceptions to the rule, of course.'

Sam snorted. 'From the woman currently sporting this season's chicest finger to elbow white plaster cast, I'm not sure you're in a position to be quite so judgemental.'

Freya looked around for something to throw, but there was nothing in her cubicle and she certainly wasn't wasting her toast, so she took another bite.

A face peered around the curtain. 'Hey, good to see you're looking better,' said Amos. 'You had us worried there for a minute.'

'Oh, I'm fine, a good clean break. If you're going to break your arm, then you could learn a thing or two from me, apparently. Besides which I'm drugged up to the eyeballs and currently don't care about anything much.'

'Ah,' said Amos, and exchanged a grin with Sam.

'Sorry, I'm being mean, of course I care. How did you get on without me?'

'Well, mistletoe sold, check. Holly sold, check. Wreaths all sold, check, check, check. You got an alarmingly good price for those; I think the punters were feeling sorry for you.'

'So it was worth it then, breaking my arm? That's a relief.' Freya grinned.

Sam looked down at his body. 'I know I wouldn't have got the sympathy vote, but I don't suppose you noticed if we managed to sell anything, did you? That is of course if Stephen even realised the auction had started.'

'No, you're good too, don't worry. I'm not sure what price yours fetched, but it all went. I've left Stephen in the pub, but we can go home once you've finished your toast, Freya. The auction yard shut, so I had to move your van, but we can drop you back there first, Sam. It was good of you to stay with Freya.'

'It was good of you to stay at the sale, Amos, thank you.'

Amos dipped his head and smiled.

'But what on earth am I going to do next week?' asked Freya, suddenly panic-stricken. 'I can't make up my wreaths like this, or cut any mistletoe, and there's still all the packing to do.'

'One thing at a time,' soothed Amos. 'One thing at a time. Let's get you home first.'

'Yes, come on Sherbert, eat up. If we leave it any longer, Stephen will be that drunk, I'll be sorely tempted to leave him behind.'

Sherbert. Now that was a name Freya hadn't heard in a long time.

★ ★ ★

It's funny how food you don't have to make yourself always tastes better. It was late afternoon by the time they got home, and as the light faded, Amos put the chickens to bed and lit the fire for the evening, closing the curtains and locking out the night. Now Freya was propped up on the sofa with a mug of tea and two thick slices of cheese on toast. Her head was spinning. There were so many thoughts crowded in there, and try as she might, she couldn't get the carousel to stop. She lay back on the cushions for a moment and closed her eyes. She opened them again when she became aware that Amos was looking at her.

'Things catching up with you?'

She gave a wan smile. 'A bit, yes.'

'Then can I make a suggestion . . . ? Finish your supper and then get yourself off to bed or make one up on the sofa here in front of the fire. Take some painkillers and try to get some sleep. Everything else can wait.'

She opened her mouth to argue and then closed it again, the thought of climbing into bed was heavenly. 'You must be tired too?' she said.

'Well, it's not often my days see that much excitement, it's true, but I'll be right as rain in the morning. You, however, might feel like you've been hit by a truck.'

Freya's eyes widened. 'Thanks for that.'

'So what's it going to be, the bed or the sofa?'

'I'll just have a bit of a sleep here I think, but you don't have to make yourself scarce, Amos. Put the TV on or something, I won't mind.'

When she woke several hours later, the TV was quiet, and the room in darkness save for the low flickering of the fire. She shifted slightly, trying to get some relief from the pain in her arm, which was now throbbing nicely, and let her eyes become accustomed to the gloom. She could just make out the shape of Amos lying fast asleep on the rug in front of the fire. He'd pulled a throw from the armchair and balled it up to use as a pillow. She watched his rhythmic breathing for a while and let it lull her gently back to sleep.

7

It was the smell of bacon wafting through the house that woke her the next morning, throwing her into confusion for a minute until she worked out where she was. She was still in her clothes, and what's worse had no idea how to get out of them. She moved her legs to the edge of the sofa and inched them over the side, using her right arm to pull herself forward into a sitting position. So far so good; a few tweaks but nothing like the pain she'd experienced yesterday. She sat for a moment wondering if it was safe to stand up.

Her legs felt like wibbly jelly for some reason, but she made it to the kitchen, largely by clinging to the line of the wall down the corridor. The radio was playing softly in the background, and from the pantry, she could hear Amos murdering her favourite seasonal song, 'Fairy Tale of New York'. A pan was sizzling gently on the cooker. She sat down at the table with an audible sigh and lay her head on her right arm with her eyes shut.

'I know I'm being selfish and whiny, but could you please turn down the chirpiness this morning?' she asked.

Amos walked back past her saying nothing, but the singing stopped. There were sounds of an egg being cracked into a pan and then a soft expletive as the oil spat. A few moments later, a deliciously smelling plate of food was placed in front of her, together with a mug of tea. Her stomach gave a lurch of appreciation.

'Are you trying to fatten me up even more?' She smiled, lifting her head.

'At the risk of perjuring myself, I shall refrain from answering that question.'

'Sam! What are you doing here?' exclaimed Freya, looking around the kitchen. 'I thought you were Amos.'

Sam chuckled and sat down. 'He's out with Bailey. He seems to have struck up rather a friendship with my horse, and anyone who offers to save me from my early morning mucking out duties gets their arm bitten off. So I'm on the break-fast-making rota.'

Freya nodded, taking a huge bite of her sandwich. Egg oozed over her fingers. With only one hand to hold the door stop, her control of it was woefully inadequate.

'This is going to be messy, sorry,' she apologised. Sam merely pushed her plate closer to her.

'Are you not going to have anything?' she asked after a few moments' more contented chewing.

'I've already eaten. I was up a bit earlier than you.'

'Hmm. What is the time?'

'Just after eight.' Sam smiled, amused at her horrified expression. 'Don't worry. We've got a while to go yet before we have to panic.'

'Have you any idea how much I have to do today?'

'Yes,' said Sam, leaning forward. 'Which is why I'm here. Have you any idea how long it takes to get up in the morning when your arm is in plaster?'

Freya stared at him for a moment

and then looked away embarrassed. 'I'm sorry,' she muttered.

'I'm just teasing you. It's no bother me being here, honestly, and Amos thought you might need some help. He surmised that I might have more experience of helping young ladies remove their clothing than he has.'

'You didn't tell him, did you?'

Sam studied her for a moment. 'No, I didn't tell him, although I would say that nothing much gets past Amos. I can see it still bothers you, though, so I certainly won't mention anything.'

To her surprise, Freya's eyes filled with tears. 'Sam, don't please, I feel bad enough as it is at the moment without having to think about what I did.'

He looped his fingers under hers gently. 'Don't keep hating yourself, Freya, it was never your fault.'

She looked up at him then, her eyes dark, and shook her head.

'So . . . Amos is a bit of a find, isn't he?' he said, clearly trying to change to subject. 'I've not seen him around here before; where did he come from?'

'I don't know, actually,' sniffed Freya. 'I wouldn't be surprised if it was from under a mulberry bush. He appeared one day wanting a glass of water and somehow he just stayed.' She stared at her sandwich in speculation. 'I think he'd been working somewhere locally, and I know I should have asked around a bit before I let him in, but it never occurred to me, to be honest. It still hasn't. It's not that he actually evades answering any questions about himself, but somehow, he avoids them. I know next to nothing about him, but I'd trust him with my life.'

'Curious.'

'It's mad is what it is, but someone clearly thought I needed his help and sent him to me, that's all I can think. Of course I could be completely wrong, and by January, I'll be in small pieces under the patio.'

Sam laughed. 'I don't think so.'

'No, neither do I,' said Freya with finality. 'Right then, I can't put it off any longer. I need to go and have a wash and get changed, and while I think I've figured out most things, I cannot for the life of me see how I'm going to get my bra off. So, if you don't mind, and without looking, commenting, or laughing, please could you just unhook me at the back, and I'll take it from there.'

* * *

Sam was right, it did take a huge amount of time to get ready, and she'd just about lost the will to live by the time she'd finished. How on earth was she supposed to do all the things she needed to; and Christmas was in just over two weeks' time. The very thought of it made her want to go and lie down in a darkened room.

By the time she got back downstairs, both Sam and Amos were sitting at the table, a large notepad in front of them.

'We need a plan,' Amos said the minute he spotted her.

'I need a double brandy,' she countered.

Both men smiled.

'Not such a bad idea,' said Sam. 'Maybe just a teeny bit early, though. Shall we see if we can make it to lunchtime, at least?'

Freya stuck out her tongue.

'Right,' said Amos in purposeful fashion. 'We need to make a list of what needs doing and by when. Also, what tasks Freya can still do and those that she'll have trouble with. That way we can assign everyone specific jobs so that as far as possible we don't lose any time. Oh, and Stephen sends his best wishes, by the way.'

'Yeah right,' Freya snorted. 'The only thing that man will be concerned about is which arm I've broken, and whether I'll still be able to sign the contracts on this place.'

Sam looked at the table, and Freya could have kicked herself. She must stop doing this. She'd thought about it last night, and although she would cheerfully run Stephen over in her van, she was pleased that Sam would be part of the equation at Appleyard; she knew he would take good care of it for her.

'Well, the first priorities just at the minute are the wreaths and other decorations. They're due to be delivered again on Saturday, which gives us three days. Fortunately, I have all the wreath bases and other additions here, but nothing is wired up, and Amos you know how long that takes. It's lucky my right hand is still okay, but I'm really not sure that I can manage the wiring even so.'

'If things were already wired, could you manage to get them in the wreaths?' asked Sam. 'If you show us how, perhaps Amos and I could do that bit for you?'

'I'll need more holly and mistletoe cutting as well.'

Amos nodded. 'Sam and I have already discussed that, so it's not a problem. We can get what you need for the wreaths to start with and then harvest the last of the mistletoe later.'

'But what about your own mistletoe, Sam?' asked Freya.

He shrugged. 'It'll get done, I'm not that fussed really.'

His tone suggested that she shouldn't argue, and that was the last thing Freya wanted to do. There was one thing she wanted to know, though.

'Why are you doing all this for me, both of you — and please don't think I'm not grateful. You know that's not the case, but I have only broken my arm, and I will manage. It's nearly Christmas, and you both must have a million and one other things to be doing or places to be?'

Amos looked at Sam, who looked back at him. 'Because it's Christmas, Freya, season of goodwill to all men,' he said.

'And all women,' added Sam.

Freya sighed, she could see she wasn't going to get anything out of either of them.

'I also need a ton of shopping, a few Christmas presents and to pack up the contents of the house. That is of course once I've sorted it all out.'

'Okay . . .' said Sam slowly, 'so what shall we do tomorrow?'

'Oh ha bloody ha,' retorted Freya, and then clapped a hand to her face.

'Oh God, I forgot to order more boxes. I meant to do it at the weekend.'

'Well, I don't think we're going to be twiddling our thumbs, are we?' Amos grinned. 'Those of us that can anyway. Can I suggest that first, I make another pot of tea, and then, Freya, you can get on the internet and order more boxes. Once we've done that, perhaps we can have a lesson in wiring up the stuff for the wreaths and see whether we're any good at it. The rest we'll take as it comes.

★ ★ ★

It didn't help that Freya got a fit of the giggles and then could hardly speak, let alone demonstrate the art of bow making, but they established very quickly that Sam had two left hands. Amos, on the other hand, was a very neat worker, and after a few more practice runs, Freya was happy that he could carry on by himself.

'I think you must be my fairy Godmother.' She laughed, taking up a bow and trying to fix it in Amos' hair. She couldn't of course with only one hand, and so it slipped to one side where eventually it tangled in his curls coquettishly above one ear. Amos said nothing but simply carried on working.

'So, having established that I'm spectacularly shite at this, does that mean I've drawn the short straw and get to sort out the crap in the attic?' asked Sam.

'It does I'm afraid. The boxes won't be delivered until tomorrow, but there's a huge amount of stuff I can probably throw away from up there. Might as well make a start now. You'll need your coat, though, it's freezing up there.'

'Oh deep joy.'

Amos watched them go with a smile on his face. There were occasions when two was definitely preferable to three.

* * *

Freya was right, it was freezing up in the attic, but the room was amazing — full of crap, but still amazing. It ran the whole length of the house and was lit by five huge windows all set into the eaves, three at the front and two at the back. As an attic, it served its function very well, but Sam could see that the scope for it to become other things was huge. Their own house was pretty impressive, but it had none of the charm and comfort of Appleyard, and after Stephen had finished ripping out most of the ground floor to make a showcase open plan area, there were also very few private spaces. This would make a brilliant workroom; the light was fantastic. He watched Freya walking around disconsolately and thrust his feelings down as far as they would go.

'It's a bit daunting, isn't it,' she said. 'I don't know where to start.'

'Well, I'm yours to command, so pick a corner, and we'll work our way along. Do you want to sit down?'

'I'll be fine for a bit, I think. I might be warmer anyway, moving around.' They hadn't been able to get Freya's coat on, so instead she had a throw from the lounge tied around her. 'If we make a bit of space over on this wall first, we can stack the things that can go. Do we need a separate pile for charity shop donations do you think, as opposed to things that are just plain rubbish?'

Sam groaned. 'I knew you were going to say that; typical woman hoarder.'

'I am not!' retorted Freya. She made her way over to a tall chest of drawers that was standing to the far left. 'See, for example everything in here is just old clothes — jumpers and stuff — but there's nothing wrong with any of it.'

'So why don't you wear them then?'

'Well, most of it doesn't fit any more, and they're ancient and really old-fashioned now.'

Sam said nothing. The silence stretched out while Freya stared at him until a small smile tugged at the corners of his mouth.

'. . . Oh right, okay, I get it. It's rubbish, let's just chuck it.'

'Ruthless, that's what we've got to be, ruthless. Repeat after me?'

After an hour and a half, they had systematically cleared a whole side, emptying cupboards and boxes, until only the furniture itself remained, or things that Freya really wanted to keep and which could now be wrapped up and packed properly. Sam kept checking on her from time to time, but she seemed to be coping well with the removal of things which must hold a lot of memories for her. He pulled another box towards him into a clear space and tugged open the flaps. At first, he couldn't make out what was inside; it seemed to be just a bundle of cloths until he pulled out a tunic covered in upholstery tassels and trimming, made from the brocade of an old curtain. He knew it was an old curtain because up until he'd been about ten, it had hung in his dining room.

He held it up to get a better look. 'Jesus,' he said, laughing, 'I can't believe you still have these.'

Freya, who was sitting on a trunk leafing through an old book, turned to have a look. 'Is that what I think it is?' She grinned.

'It certainly is. Romeo, Romeo, where

106

for art thou, Romeo,' he squeaked in a high-pitched falsetto. 'Oh, no, sorry that's your line.' He cleared his throat, lowering his tone to a gruff deep voice instead. 'But Soft! What light through yonder window breaks.'

He reached back into the box, pulling out an elaborate headdress. 'Here you go, Juliet, try that on for size.'

She leaned over to take the feathered monstrosity, plonking it on top of her head. 'I can't believe we never made it to Broadway. I mean, we were good, weren't we; really good?'

'Well, your dad said so, and he never told a lie,' replied Sam, with a twinkle in his eye. 'The summer holidays had a lot to answer for.'

'Oh I think this was one of our slightly better schemes. Although I'm not sure taking our three-man plays on a nation-wide tour was ever going to truly catch on. I think, as performers, we were much misunderstood.'

'How old were we then?' He grinned.

Freya narrowed her eyes, looking at

Sam intently. 'It was 1992, and we were twelve.'

He was surprised. 'You can remember the year?'

'Don't you? That's why there were only three of us. It was the year Merry got glandular fever and spent practically the whole summer in bed. It was the year after we went up to secondary school.'

'Oh God . . . yes, you're right . . . and Stephen spent two days in a huff because I got to play Romeo and not him. We had to let him play every other part in the whole play, and the only way he could do it was to wear all the costumes at once.'

'I'd forgotten that bit,' hooted Freya. 'And then, in the one of the rehearsals he couldn't get his tights off and spent the whole of the next scene with them around his ankles. He got so mad at us because we couldn't stop laughing.'

Sam shook his head, smiling as he remembered the hilarity that had engulfed them as children. 'It could have been yesterday, couldn't it?'

'Twenty-three years ago, Sam, that's

what it was,' said Freya softly. 'Half a lifetime ago.'

He looked up at her, noticing the change in the tone of her voice. 'Still, good times, Freya.'

She swallowed. 'Yes, they were.' Her eyes filled with tears. 'I'm sorry,' she muttered, brushing at her eyes. 'It's just that —'

Sam was there, by her side, holding her hand. 'I know,' he said gently. 'I feel it too.'

She shivered all of a sudden. 'I don't think I need to keep the costumes,' she said in a quiet voice, slowly withdrawing her hand.

He held her look for just a second before pulling the hat from her head and stuffing it back into the box with the tunic. He gave a quick glance at his watch.

'Another hour or so, and then we'll think about stopping for some lunch. Is that okay?'

Freya nodded. 'I think these boxes are full of old toys and stuff. They can pretty much all go, I think.'

★ ★ ★

Amos placed a teapot on the table as Freya lowered herself gingerly onto a chair. He took one look at her and fetched the painkillers from the dresser. Sam was only seconds behind with a plate of beans on toast.

'Sorry, we should have stopped before now.'

Freya gave a wan smile. 'It's fine really, I'll be okay in a bit once I've taken some of these. It's only just crept up on me, now we've stopped. Besides, it was good to get that last bit finished.'

'It was, we've done well this morning.' He handed her a fork. 'Go on, eat up before it gets cold,' he said, taking a seat too. 'I've cut it up for you.'

'Thanks, Sam.' Freya smiled. 'This looks good enough to eat.'

Sam glanced at Amos and rolled his eyes.

'I can't believe you got so much done this morning, Amos,' added Freya, looking at the pile of greenery and ribbon

110

which they had pushed to one end of the table. 'I think I'll be able to get quite a few wreaths made up with that lot.'

'Well, I was on a bit of a roll,' admitted Amos. 'I enjoyed it actually; it's quite soothing once you get into the rhythm of it. Good thinking time.'

'Oh — and what were you thinking about?' asked Freya, being nosey.

Amos tapped the side of his nose. 'This and that,' he said, 'nothing important. I do have a favour to ask, though? I wondered if I might borrow your iPad for five minutes later. I want to check something on the internet.'

'Of course, just help yourself whenever. There's nothing incriminating on there, unless you count my appallingly bad score on Candy Crush. It's not locked either.'

Amos nodded his thanks and carried on eating.

Freya had to admit that she did feel better after the food, but she wasn't sure she could face another session up in the attic. Things had been just a little too close to home at times.

'Shall we get rid of the rubbish before we carry on, do you think?'

'Amos and I will do that,' said Sam. 'You're going to put your feet up for a bit. And don't argue,' he continued, seeing the look on her face. 'There's no point killing yourself on the first day. Besides which I need to run a few errands while we're out.'

They'd already done two laborious journeys with armfuls of stuff before Freya realised what they were doing. She straightened up from the dishwasher where she was stacking the last of the plates.

'Erm, how are you going to get all that stuff to the tip?' she asked.

Sam looked at her as if she were deranged. 'In the van,' he said slowly.

'Yes, I know that, but it doesn't matter how it gets there, does it? I mean you're just going to throw it all in higgledy piggledy?'

Sam scratched his head. 'Pretty much,' he said, clearly wondering if there was any other way.

'Okay, come with me.' She led the way back upstairs, passing Amos on the landing with another load. 'About turn,' she said, 'and bring that lot with you.'

'No, I haven't got a clue what she's talking about either,' muttered Sam, 'but I would do as she says.'

Back in the attic, Freya crossed to one of the large windows overlooking the front lawn. The van was parked in the yard, neatly to one side.

'Could one of you open the window please?'

Sam and Amos exchanged more looks, but Amos did as she asked, moving the catch on the sash and pushing the window up as far as it would go.

'Now just throw.'

'Pardon?' said Amos.

'It's a hell of a lot quicker than carrying it all down two flights of stairs. Just throw. It's all rubbish anyway, what harm is it going to do?'

'You're mad,' grinned Sam, 'but I kind of like your thinking. Wheelbarrow to the van at the other end, done in a flash.' He picked up an armful of clothing and hurled it out of the window. 'That's strangely satisfying.' He laughed.

'Ruthless you said,' fired back Freya. 'So I give you ruthless.' And with that, she left them to it, smiling to herself all the way downstairs as she listened to the gales of laughter floating after her.

★ ★ ★

Freya was still asleep by the time they got back, right where Sam had left her, tucked up under a blanket on the sofa. He'd put *Love Actually* on the DVD before he left, but it had long since finished, the final credits frozen onto the silent screen. He watched her for a moment, his eyes soft in the dim light, before rejoining Amos in the kitchen.

'Did you find what you were looking for?' he asked. Amos' head was bent over the iPad.

'Yeah, getting there. Just looking at a

few things. Does the name Paul Streatfield mean anything to you?'

Sam came to sit beside him so that he could see the screen. 'I don't think so, why?'

'It's just a name I've heard your brother use a few times now, that's all. It pricked my interest.'

'Who is he, anyway?' asked Sam.

'A property developer — look.' Amos angled the screen towards Sam so that he could get a better look.

Sam pulled the iPad closer and studied it for a moment before gazing back at Amos and echoing his worried frown.

'Shit,' he said.

8

It was Sam's idea to visit Worcester, but while Freya could see the logic in it, she wasn't sure she really wanted to be here. There were too many reminders of Christmases past tugging at her brain.

It was three in the afternoon by the time they arrived, having dropped off her wreaths at the hotel first. That had taken rather longer than planned since Merry and Tom insisted they stay for lunch. Merry declared that it was the least she could do since her pregnant state meant she'd been unable to help Freya pack. Hospitality was what they did best, and as Freya looked around the hotel at the other guests enjoying a sumptuous pre-Christmas break, she could see the appeal.

The reception hall was a glittery double height room, dominated by the huge tree which was smothered in white and gilded sparkles. A marble fireplace roaring with flame enticed people onto the squishy deep red sofas, in front of which a table groaned with plates of mince pies, sugar-dusted shortbread and a tower of Ferrero Rocher. Sitting in the dining room, chatting with old friends, it was easy to forget everything else for a while and let Christmas wash over her, an oasis of seasonal charm.

When they finally reached it, the town was still thronging with people. The day was cold and clear, and as they emerged from beside the cathedral, the lights and sounds from the shops drifted over to them. Instead of following the road into town, Sam steered Freya away to the left and through the elegant Cathedral close to the quieter riverside beyond. As they walked through the arch that lead onto the path beside the river, Freya looked at the markers on the huge wall beside them showing the height the river had reached when in flood. It amazed her that some of them were ten feet or so above her head and they were already standing maybe twenty feet above the river itself. It was an important reminder that despite the torrents of life, things endured, maybe not unaltered, but they remained, nonetheless. Right now, when everything she held dear seemed to be slipping away from her, it was hard to see how things could ever get back to even a slight semblance of what they had been before.

Sam took hold of her hand, perhaps sensing how she was feeling, or just wanting to provide support as she walked. His hand was warm and solid, and the feeling of it was as familiar to her as breathing. It would be so easy to allow her feelings to drift back in time, but she knew that Sam was only being friendly, marking time until she left, and finally gave him the closure she had never allowed him before. She should have pulled away, but she was so tired it was somehow easier just to hang on.

She tried to enjoy the chilly air and let her mind drift away from the reality of her current problems, but everywhere she looked tiny sparkles of fairy lights caught her eye and brought her back to the one thing she was dreading. Christmas. She usually loved it all: the shops decked out way before time, the Christmas music playing over and over and the cheesy films on the TV. Most of all, though, she loved the lights; the darkened villages and houses transformed at dusk into winter wonderlands of colour. She loved this over-spilling of joy and exuberance, and although it had only ever been her and her dad at home, she had always strung rows and rows of lights through Appleyard. Until this year.

She walked a little closer to Sam, his thick puffy jacket warm to the touch. The sky was turning violet as the day gave way to dusk, and the lights were beginning to glow off the river. They had walked the whole way in virtual silence and Freya felt no need to talk, but soon they would be heading back into town, and the thought brought her back to the reason for their visit.

'Where would you like to go?' she asked Sam.

He too seemed lost in his own thoughts,

and it took him a little while to respond. 'I'll follow you,' he said. 'Wherever you want to go. I can shop any time after all.'

That was undoubtedly true, but when Freya tried to think what she might need to buy, she realised she had no stomach for shopping; she had wanted to come and soak up the atmosphere because it was something she always did, and without it she would feel even more lost. In truth, there was only one shop she wanted to visit, but she was loathe to name it for fear of seeming even more of a sentimental fool.

'Can we just wander and see what happens?'

'No problem,' said Sam, falling silent beside her once more.

They made their way up from the bridge into the town centre, weaving through the crowds into the market square, where the huge Christmas tree stood over the market stalls, ablaze with lights. A Salvation Army band was still playing, and the brass notes rang out rich and clear. She stopped to listen, noting that Sam too had slowed his pace.

'Wouldn't be Christmas without them, would it?' He smiled, fishing in his pocket for some change. 'I could listen to them for hours.'

'Me too. I don't know why, but they always bring a lump to my throat. I think it's the thought that amid all the horrible things that happen in this world, there are still people like them who help, without question, without judgement. That's what I like about Christmas, the reminder that there is still good in the world. Sometimes, it seems so far away.'

'There are still good people in the world, Freya,' he said.

'I know,' she said, moving her fingers in his, and blinking away her tears.

They stood listening for a few moments more, then Sam pulled her gently away, leading her to a stall selling nuts of every variety coated in delicious sounding ingredients, savoury and sweet. Sam bought some spiced honey cashews which they munched from the twisted cone of paper, each time Freya dropping Sam's hand to take one, and each time reuniting it with his.

She almost didn't go into the shop at all. She thought if she kept walking and didn't think about it, then it would be fine, but suddenly the thought of not going in became too much to bear, and she pushed the door open almost with reverence. The first few moments as she stood inside were always the same; that first rush of excitement and endless possibility looming up at her as she stared at every manner of bauble and decoration, assailed by the shapes and colours, the sheer variety. She and her dad would wander around at first, in no particular direction, he going one way and she the other, and then they would meet up for an excited exchange of what the other had seen. Eventually, they would gravitate towards one of the displays as if drawn by an invisible thread, and the selection would begin in earnest. They had bought a new Christmas decoration together every year since her mum had left. It was their special bond, a celebration of another year, and although she wasn't going to decorate the house this year, it was a tradition that she simply couldn't bring to an end. Whatever she bought would remain on her bedside table until it too was packed away.

Almost as soon as they were through the door, Sam dropped her hand and headed off to take a closer look at something that had caught his eye. The shop wasn't busy now, and she was happy to wander alone, pleased to find that the usual sense of wonderment she felt on coming inside was still with her.

She had paused by a display of neon decorations, which were gaudy but strangely attractive when she became aware that Sam was hovering by her side.

'This place is amazing,' he said. 'How did you find it?'

'I can't remember, just stumbled across it one year. It's only here at Christmas of course, the rest of the year it sells giftware.'

'Are you going to buy something?'

'I'd like to . . . it's sort of a tradition.'

Sam gave an understanding nod. 'How on earth do you choose, though?'

'I don't know really. The one I want seems to find me.'

'Okay, well happy hunting.' He grinned at her and wandered off again.

Freya had only moved a little way around the corner when he was back again, almost fizzing with excitement.

'You need to come over here,' he urged, and grabbed her hand, not caring about the other shoppers in their path.

They were near the back of the shop now, standing in front of a small section of more expensive decorations, all made from the most beautiful glass, a myriad of colours and sizes. Her eyes scanned this way and that, and then she saw it, seconds before Sam's hand reached out to take it gingerly down from its hiding place. It was about the size of an apple, a handmade glass ornament of pale cranberry glass, a single perfect white feather curled within it in perfect suspension. Her breath caught in her throat as she reached out a trembling hand to take it.

'What do you think?' asked Sam anxiously.

Freya held her breath, hardly daring to move. 'I can't believe you found it,' she said, her voice choked with emotion. 'This is it; this is absolutely it.' She turned to him, her eyes shining. 'How did you know?'

'I didn't, I saw it . . . and it just seemed . . . right. Like the sort of thing you should have.'

Freya was still gazing at the ornament in her hand. 'Can we buy it?' she asked, handing it back to him. 'Is it very expensive?'

Sam cleared his throat which felt a little constricted. 'It's twenty pounds. I'm sorry, I should have checked the price first, but Freya . . . ' He faltered for a moment, trying to find the right words, 'I want you to have this . . . I'd like to buy it for you . . . please.'

She paused for a moment, but then to his surprise, she gave a slight nod. 'I'd like that,' she said, looking up at him. 'Because then I'll have something to remember you too.' And she did something she'd sworn she'd never do again. She kissed him.

* * *

'I don't want to sound rude, Amos, but I was wondering what your plans for Christmas were?'

Amos looked up from his book and gave her a warm smile. 'Not rude at all,' he said. 'It's a busy time of year, only natural that you would want to know.' He placed his bookmark back in the book and laid it on his lap. 'I've been thinking about it too as it happens, and I thought maybe I would go at the end of the week if that's all right with you? The work will pretty much be done by then, and there's heavy snow coming in after.'

'Is there?' Freya replied, surprised. 'I hadn't heard that . . . but . . . what I meant was more, well, whether you had definite plans, that sort of thing. Do you have somewhere you're meant to be?'

Amos considered the question for a

moment. 'No, nowhere I'm meant to be, but often the place I am, well, it's the same thing.'

Freya grinned, giving an amused tut at his enigmatic answer. She was beginning to expect nothing less from him. 'Good, because what I really meant was, if you don't have to be anywhere in particular, would you like to stay here for Christmas? It won't be very grand because everything will be in boxes, but I'd like it if you were here.'

'Then I accept,' replied Amos. 'Thank you. I didn't like the thought of you being here by yourself. It didn't seem right.'

Freya stared into the fire for a moment. 'No, me neither,' she said finally, giving a huge yawn. 'I might head up to bed now actually. I'm so tired, and it's going to take me an age to get ready anyway.'

'Do you need anything?'

'No, it's fine, thanks, I'll just take my book.' She eyed the glass bauble sitting on the mantelpiece.

'I could bring it up for you if you like?' ventured Amos, watching her.

She smiled again. 'Sorry, I just thought I might have it beside my bed.'

'Then that's where you shall have it.'

When her head eventually met the pillow, she lay for a few moments looking at the bauble, lost in thought. This morning she had wished that she could be on her own for Christmas. She had thought she wanted nothing more than to see out the last few days at Appleyard by herself so that she could say her own goodbyes, but something had changed during the course of the day. She'd realised it in the car driving home earlier that afternoon, and she was trying desperately hard not to admit it to herself. Perhaps having Amos stay would help to keep the thoughts chasing around her head at bay. Perhaps. She closed her eyes and willed sleep to come and claim her.

9

'And here's another festive treat for this fine Monday morning to get you in the mood. After all, the big day is now only four away.'

Sam switched off the radio irritably, he didn't need any more bloody reminders of how little time he had left. The last week or so had passed in a blur. He drained his coffee mug and stared morosely at the toaster. He was due back at Appleyard tomorrow to help with more packing, and although he had no great expectations of the day, at least it meant he wouldn't have to suffer Stephen's smug comments at home. He could hear him now, arguing on the phone with someone. It was only nine o'clock in the morning, for God's sake.

He concentrated on buttering his toast, trying to ignore his brother's strident tones as they grew louder. Stephen was still a little wary around him since getting punched, but it didn't stop him from reminding Sam at every given opportunity that he would soon own Appleyard too.

'Have a heart, mate, even the wankers — sorry, bankers — don't work at the weekend. I'm doing the best I can. My man's on it, believe me, and I'm expecting to hear from him later today.' Stephen paused for a moment, nodding intermittently. 'Yes, of course, I will, cheers, Paul.'

He ended the call, pulling an exasperated face at Sam. 'That man has no bloody idea, but you have to keep 'em sweet, don't you?'

'Do you?' countered Sam. 'I really wouldn't know,' he added, feigning disinterest, although the mention of the name Paul had caught his ear. He knew better than to quiz his brother, though; that was the quickest way to get him to clam up.

'Course I wouldn't have a problem if your doe-eyed little girlfriend wasn't being quite so picky.'

Sam said nothing, but his eyes glittered dangerously.

'Oh, of course, she's not your girl-friend, is she, sorry.' Stephen smirked. 'Anyway, give her a message from me, would you? Tell her to pull her socks up on the sale; we're running out of time. Her bloody solicitor won't progress until he has written confirmation of the mortgage offer, and we haven't got time to be pissing around.'

'That's standard practice I believe, Stephen. Haven't you done your home-work?'

Stephen swiped a piece of toast. 'Just bloody tell her,' he growled, and stalked off.

Sam allowed a small smile to curl around the corners of his lips; he liked to see his brother riled, especially when it forced him to show his cards. He hadn't known until now that Stephen needed a mortgage to buy Appleyard; which was interesting. For the first time in a long time, he saw a way that he might just be able to outmanoeuvre his brother. He would call his solicitor as soon as Stephen was out of the way.

10

Amos and Freya had already made good progress by the time Sam got there, having sorted another whole section of the attic. When he found them, Freya was holding up some threadbare tinsel that had discoloured to a diseased-looking green. She held it between thumb and forefinger in case whatever it had was catching.

'When you said you weren't going to bother putting up the decorations, I thought you were being boring, now I can see why. That's pretty disturbing.'

'Morning, Sam.' Freya laughed. 'It is, isn't it? I think the box must have got damp, it's all like this which is a shame because I was looking forward to putting these out.' She fished inside the box and pulled out two very moth-eaten-looking reindeer, which at one time in their lives had been furry but now had a severe case of alopecia. 'I'd forgotten we even had them.'

'Blanked it from your memory probably,' said Sam with a shudder. 'Stuff of nightmares.'

'Look, are you going to stand there criticising my family heirlooms, or make yourself useful and cart this lot over there with the rest of the rubbish?'

'Yes, ma'am,' grinned Sam, picking up a box. 'Being serious for a minute, though, are you going to put anything up this year? It seems such a shame not to do anything, especially as tomorrow is Mistletoe Day.'

'But it's just one more thing to have to do, when I could leave it all in its boxes, ready and packed.'

'It wouldn't take long . . . and we'd help, wouldn't we, Amos?'

'Oh for heaven's sake, you're as bad as him,' she said, pointing a finger. 'Okay, you win. Take the stuff downstairs and leave it in the dining room, and then I can decide. It's those boxes over there,' she added, wafting her good hand at a pile by the door.

Sam did as he was told, a plan forming in his mind.

The dining room was stacked high with boxes already packed, and it took a few minutes to move the others around to make way for those coming down. He was trying hard not to think about what they meant, and how little time he had left. He pulled his mobile out of his pocket as it buzzed with a message. It was from his brother, three words in block capitals.

CALL ME NOW

Sam clicked the sleep button, watching with satisfaction as the screen went dark again. *Oops*, he said to himself. *I missed that one*.

He was just moving the last few boxes when Amos appeared with another couple.

'These are all decorations too,' he said, putting them down where Sam indicated. 'Just in case they're needed at all,' he added, winking. 'You must tell me about the customs of Mistletoe Day some time. It sounds fascinating.'

Sam laughed. 'As if you didn't know. You don't fool me, Amos Fry.'

'And you don't fool me either, Sam Henderson.' Amos grinned. 'One other thing, though. Can I suggest that we go and get the shopping fairly soon, there's snow coming, and I don't think we should leave it too late.'

The day outside was clear and blue, just as it had been for days. 'I know it's nearly Christmas, but that doesn't mean it's going to start snowing. Have you looked outside?'

'Yes, and I know that snow hasn't actually been forecast.'

'But?'

Amos winked again. 'I tell you it's coming.'

'Okaaay,' said Sam, humouring him. 'Let's go and grab the rest of these boxes, and then we'll see about putting a list together. Not because I believe a word you're saying about the snow, but because the supermarket will be like your worst nightmare, and I'd rather not leave it any longer.'

* * *

Sam had a total of four more text messages and two missed calls by the time they eventually emerged from the supermarket hours later. Freya had wanted to come, but Sam insisted she stayed at home. There would be too many people around all pushing and shoving, and he thought she'd find it very uncomfortable. Instead, she had provided them with a list that made the Declaration of Independence look like a scribbled note on the back of a napkin. The list contained things that neither Sam nor Amos had ever heard of, but they had been determined to find everything she asked for.

Now, with the bags stashed safely in the boot, Sam pulled out his phone to look at the messages again and tried to concentrate. The texts were all from his brother, more shouty messages, getting more ridiculously threatening by the minute. Sam had no intention of answering them. This was not his battle to fight he had decided; not this time. He had assumed that the missed call was also from Stephen, but although there was no message left, he recognised the number, and checking Amos was okay to wait, he returned the call.

'That was good news I take it?' said Amos, looking at the Cheshire cat grin on Sam's face.

'The very best,' he replied. 'Do you mind if we make a quick detour on the way home? There's one last shop I need to visit. Got my Christmas present to pick up.'

Amos glanced at the sky. 'No problem, we've still got time.'

The High Street was packed with people, but by some miracle, Sam managed to find a parking spot in a side street and nipped out to finish his shopping.

'I won't be long, I promise.'

It was gone three o'clock by the time they navigated their way out of the car-choked streets and began to head for home. They were only a couple of miles into their journey when Sam took his sunglasses off. The late sun, hanging low in the sky made visibility particularly difficult at this time of year, and he never went anywhere without them. Now, though, he realised he was having trouble seeing, not because of the glare, but because of the sudden reduction in light. He dipped his head to look below the sun visor, shaking his head as he did so. The sky was split in two; one half still the brightest winter blue, and the other banked with dark clouds sporting an ominous pink tinge.

'I don't bloody believe it,' he remarked, driving on.

As he drove, the line of cloud sank lower and lower to the ground, and by the time they turned into the driveway at Appleyard, the first flakes of snow were falling.

'So what is it with you then, Amos? Got a direct line to the big man upstairs or what?'

Amos gave him an innocent look.

'Don't give me that, you know what I'm talking about, the whole "snow is coming" thing.'

'My bones have been around longer than yours, that's all.' He grinned. 'They sense these things.'

'Bullshit!' said Sam succinctly, and jumped out of the car to haul the first of the shopping inside.

Freya was chopping vegetables by the sink, or at least she was trying to. She had pinned a carrot to a board with her cast and was slowly making progress with her good hand. She looked up as they came in.

'I got bored sifting through the papers upstairs, so I thought I'd make a start on tea. It's taken me rather longer than I thought, though.'

'Interesting technique,' said Sam.

'But strangely effective, so don't mock.'

He dumped the first of the bags on the table and went to inspect the pans on top of the stove.

'That's not what I can smell, though,'

he said, lifting one of the saucepan lids, and inhaling deeply.

'No, I made some mulled wine for later too. I thought we'd have a casserole, and as it took me so long to get the wine open, I thought I might as well use it all up.'

'I like your thinking,' said Sam, 'although I wish I'd been here. I'd have paid good money to see you trying to get into a bottle of wine.'

Freya gave him an amused look. 'Yes, well, if you were clamped between my knees for that long, you'd surrender too.'

Sam turned away so that she wouldn't see the smile on his face. My, that was a vivid image.

'Right, well, I'll help Amos bring the rest of the shopping in, and then I'll give you a hand. We bought enough to feed an army.'

'Good, just what you need at Christmas: faith, hope and gluttony.'

★ ★ ★

140

'I'm not sure I should be drinking this,' said Freya, with a total lack of concern. 'Are you allowed to drink alcohol with painkillers?'

'Bit late I think,' offered Amos. 'How many glasses is that now?'

'I haven't been counting, but more than one.' She squinted up at him. 'Oh hell, never mind. I don't have to go anywhere.'

'No, but Sam does, I'm not sure it was such a good idea.'

'It's only two miles away, and at this time of night no one will be on the road. He'll be fine.'

Amos frowned at her.

'I wouldn't normally say it was okay to drink and drive,' she said, 'before you give me a lecture, but if the roads are a bit snowy, he'll have to go at a snail's pace anyway.'

She hoped she didn't sound too much like she wanted to get rid of him. She'd rather enjoyed standing side by side with him cooking their tea, the way they'd giggled at silly reminders of their childhood.

She'd also enjoyed the way he leaned into her to get her to move along the work surface a bit, and the way his green eyes lit up when he laughed. She'd enjoyed the way his hand brushed against hers as he reached for her wine glass and the affectionate way he teased her during dinner. Then she had enjoyed sneaking little glances at him as he relaxed in the chair, drowsy with wine and food, and the thought of what it might be like if he were there every night; and that was why she very much wanted him to go, because actually she didn't want him to go at all.

She sneaked a peek at Amos now, wondering just how much of herself she might be giving away, when Sam came back into the room.

'Um . . . you might want to come and have a look at this,' he said, the wool of his coat glistening with snowflakes in the room's soft light.

Freya pulled herself up out of the chair, giving him a quizzical glance and then following him through into the kitchen, where he went to stand by the back door. She could see the wet imprint of his footprints across the tiled floor.

'We've had the curtains closed all evening, and it's, well, um, snowed a bit.' He pulled the door open.

The light was on just outside the back door, throwing a small bright circle out into the night. Against the patch of lit sky, a torrent of snow was falling, thick and steady. Of the grass, path and driveway there was no sign. Even the car was just a muffled outline.

Freya peered out into the whiteness and then back at Sam. 'How the hell did that happen?' she exclaimed, turning to look at Amos.

'Why are you looking at me?' He grinned.

Freya and Sam exchanged glances. 'No reason, no reason at all.' Sam sighed. 'I could walk, I suppose?'

'You could, if you were stark raving mad,' she replied, firmly closing the door, and turning the key in the lock. 'If I show you where the linen is for the spare bed, could you help me make it up?' *Keep it businesslike*, she thought to herself, *it's the only way.*

Sam trailed after her.

'It'll be cold in here I expect, the room hasn't been used for a while, but if we put on the radiator and turn down the covers once the bed is made that should give it time to air before you turn in.'

'Listen, don't worry, I'll have another glass of wine, and then I won't feel the cold anyway.'

'I've got plenty of blankets if you need extra,' said Freya, hating herself for sounding like a Blackpool boarding house landlady. 'They're all in this drawer here, and the sheets and duvet cover. Bit pink I'm afraid.'

Sam crossed the room and looked out through the window for a moment before closing the curtains. 'No problem. I tend to sleep with my eyes closed and the light off, so I won't notice what colour they are.'

Freya snorted before she could stop herself. Oh my God, was she drunk? It wasn't even that funny. She struggled to pull the drawer open.

'Here, let me do that,' said Sam, his hand brushing against hers, again.

'Thank you ... I should just go and get you the spare duvet, it's in the airing cupboard, and if you want any more pillows, they're in the wardrobe there.'

She walked back down the landing, blowing out her cheeks in an effort to relax her face which currently felt like she'd had ten Botox injections, stiff and wooden yet strangely liquid all at the same time. She reminded herself that Sam had been in her house now for the best part of a month on and off with no problem whatsoever. That was it, she must be drunk, or hormonal, or both.

Trying to contain the duvet under one arm, she kicked open the bedroom door once more. 'Do you need anything — ' she started, and then she stopped because standing in the middle of the room was Sam, holding a wedding dress. Her wedding dress.

She hadn't a clue what to say, so she

just stood there looking at Sam, looking at her dress, looking at her.

After what seemed like an age, Sam started to apologise. 'I went to get a pillow . . . I'm sorry, I didn't know it was in there.'

Freya rubbed her forehead distractedly. 'No . . . I'd forgotten it was. It's my fault.' She could feel her eyes filling with tears, and she couldn't breathe. 'I'm so sorry,' she whispered, turning to run.

And then Sam was there, holding her, pulling her to him, stroking her hair. 'You don't have to run, Freya,' he murmured. 'Not any more. Please don't run.'

She wished with all her heart that she could believe him.

11

Mistletoe Day

Sam woke the next morning to the sound of hammering on the back door. He raised a bleary eye to the clock, suddenly sitting up as he realised the time. Pulling on his jeans, he grabbed his fleece from the chair and went to investigate. He could tell from the white glow behind the curtains that the snow was still around, so there couldn't be that many people up and about, even if it was ten o'clock.

He winced as his feet met the cold quarry tiles in the kitchen. Someone was obviously up, as the blinds had been raised, and through the windows, he could see the snow still blowing into huge drifts. He hadn't expected there to be quite so much; even as he pulled the door open, a small pile slumped inward and onto the floor. And he certainly hadn't expected to see the person who was standing there either.

His brother looked dreadful. He was obviously cold, his face looked pinched and mottled in places, his nose bright red; but his eyes were wild, bloodshot and staring. He practically fell into the kitchen.

'Why the hell aren't you answering your bloody phone?' he snarled. 'I've been ringing you all morning.'

Sam's gaze fell to the table where his phone lay exactly where he had left it last night.

'I've only just got up,' he said flatly, not in the mood for one of his brother's arguments. 'How did you get here any-way?'

'I followed the sodding snow-plough, it's taken me nearly an hour.' Stephen looked around the kitchen which still smelled faintly of last night's mulled wine. 'Can I at least have a cup of coffee?'

Sam filled the kettle, feeling a little uneasy about doing so in Freya's absence, but reasoning that it might be the quick-est way to get rid of Stephen. He slid it back onto the Aga's hotplate, and turned to face his brother.

'So where's the fire?' he said evenly.

'Don't bloody joke about. Is she here?'

Sam could feel his anger rising and did his best to stay calm. 'If you mean Freya, I haven't seen her yet this morning.'

'Oh, like I believe that. From where I'm standing, it looks as though your slippers are well and truly under the bed.'

'Yeah, well, that's what you would see when you're standing in the gutter, Stephen. For your information, I stayed last night because I'd had a drink or two, and the snow came down too heavy. It wasn't safe to go anywhere. Besides which, the company here was rather more pleasant than that at home.'

Stephen glared at him. 'Stop being such a snide little fucker, Sam, I'm not in the mood for pissing about.'

Sam glared back at him, tempted to simply throw him out, but as he stared at his brother, he was astonished to see something else in his eyes which he couldn't ever recall having seen there before. Aside from the habitual arrogant defiance, there was a glimmer of fear, and it made a shiver run down Sam's spine. He threw some coffee into a mug and stood drumming his fingers against the Aga while he waited for the kettle to boil.

'So, do you want to sit down and tell me what this is all about, or will you carry on playing the big I am, because if it's the latter, I'm going to throw you out now and save us all the bother.'

Sam could see that Stephen was treading a knife-edge here. His natural instinct would be to shout and bully to get his own way, but instead he was trying to choose his words carefully, and moderate his behaviour. It didn't come naturally to him; in his view, it was tantamount to admitting he was wrong. Whatever it was must be very important, or worse, something that he needed Sam's help with.

'I wondered whether Freya had heard from her solicitor, that's all. The timing's getting critical on the sale, and they seem to be dragging their feet.'

'Well, she hasn't mentioned it, but

then it's not something we've discussed. Under the circumstances, I don't think she feels it's a subject she can bring up.'

'Perhaps you could have a word with her, ask her to give him a ring and check that everything is in place. They'll shut down for Christmas tomorrow, and we could really do with getting it moving today.'

Sam moved the kettle off the hotplate. 'Do you really think that solicitors are going to be interested in anything today? Besides drinking sherry and eating Quality Street with their staff, that is. Stephen, everything's pretty much shut down already.' He watered the coffee and handed it to his brother.

'But you don't know that. There's a lot riding on this, Sam. I thought you might be more interested.'

'Not particularly.' Sam shrugged. 'Not any more.' He held his brother's look for a moment, trying to read him. 'What exactly is riding on this, Stephen? It's only a house sale, they happen every day; and some of them don't happen, but it's not worth getting hysterical over.'

'Are you being deliberately obtuse? For Christ's sake, Sam, I'm your brother, try to remember whose side you're on. I just need to know if the money is the only thing holding the sale up. I need her solicitor to confirm that and I need it today.'

Sam smiled then, the penny finally dropping. 'So you're having trouble getting the mortgage through then, Stephen. But why is that? You shouldn't have any problems at all I'd have thought, especially not when you're using our place as collateral.'

Stephen's gaze was fixed at the level of the table, but Sam could see his jaw working in anger. Slowly, he looked up, his face red and blotchy. 'You smug little shit,' he hissed.

Sam ignored him. 'How much, Stephen? Eh? Just how much do you owe?'

Stephen shifted slightly in his chair. 'It's just a few gambling debts, that's all. Nothing I can't handle.'

'Jesus, Stephen, when will you stop?

When will you ever learn that enough is enough? How much is it? Twenty grand? Fifty grand? . . . A hundred grand . . . ?'

'I won't owe anything if I can get this house, don't you get it?'

Sam sat down at the table, leaning closer to his brother. 'Then you'd better tell me, hadn't you,' he said, shoving his face closer still.

Something crumpled behind the façade then, and Stephen clung to the table before lowering himself onto a chair. He ran shaky hands through his hair and closed his eyes.

'I met a bloke in the pub a while back. We had a few beers and then a few more and before I knew it, he'd suggested we had a game of cards. He was an arrogant bastard, but he knew what he was doing, and at the end of the night, I owed him five hundred quid.'

'Oh, and let me guess, you thought you could beat him? Just one more game, eh?'

'They were serious guys, Sam, you wouldn't understand. They didn't just play for a few pounds, they played for big bucks, and not just cards either. It wasn't unusual to win or lose twenty grand during a night.'

'So you gambled your inheritance to get the better of some bloke down the pub. Nice one, Stephen. What did you do? Re-mortgage the house?'

'So what if I did? None of this will matter if I can get this place, everything will be okay.'

'Explain.'

Stephen rolled his eyes. 'I'm not as stupid as you think, little brother. While you were out there slaving away picking bloody apples for peanuts, I was making connections, and a couple of months ago, I hit the jackpot; a property developer who was looking for a new investment project.

Two houses, two orchards, a lot of land; it's a desirable venture for an astute businessman with money to spare.'

'Except that you don't have two houses and two orchards, do you? Only the one, and a whole heap of debt.'

154

'Which is why I need your bloody help. I need to get the sale through on this place, otherwise I'm going to lose my buyer. This is small fry for him, he won't hang around. Don't you get it, Sam? When you have that kind of money, it's just a game, and he's getting impatient.'

'But you just said you can't get a mortgage?'

'I need the funds, Sam, that's all. You could lend me the money, couldn't you? It would only be for a short while, until the sale of the whole lot goes through, and then you'll get it back twofold, I promise.'

Sam jerked his chair away from the table as he stood up sharply. 'No,' he said coldly, his mouth a thin line. 'It's about time you learned to stop playing with people's lives, Stephen. You can't have everything just because you want it; life doesn't work that way.'

'Oh, but it does, doesn't it?' bit back Stephen, his bravado returning. 'I can have everything I want, can't I? Anything of yours, that is. I can take what I like, remember?'

'Don't you dare bring Freya into this!'

'Why not? I'm not the only one making plans around here. Don't think your knight-in-shining-armour routine is fooling anyone, not for one minute.'

'And neither is your big-man, I-can-do-anything routine. You've lost this one, Stephen. Accept it.'

Stephen lurched up from the table, his face contorted with rage. 'So what the hell am I supposed to do?'

'What other people do,' replied Sam mildly. 'Act like a grown-up, get a proper job, pay your way. Take responsibility for once in your life.'

'But the people I owe money to won't take no for an answer. How am I going to pay them off now?'

'Sell the house. Settle your debts, start over.'

'Look, I don't even need your cash. You could act as guarantor on the mortgage or something. Just have a chat to the bank, Sam, please. They're the ones that have caused all this mess. It would only be for a short while and — '

'The answer's still no, Stephen. The banks have had their fingers burned too. They won't lend you the money no matter how hard you beg them to, and neither will I.'

The back door opened then, catching them both by surprise as Amos came through, stamping his feet on the mat to release the snow from his boots.

'Merry mistletoe!' He grinned at them both, holding aloft a glistening sprig. 'Morning, Stephen. I hope you're on your way back home soon. The snow's coming down again, and by the look of the sky, there's a heap more on its way. In a short while, nothing will be moving.'

Stephen glared at them both, then flung his chair back under the table with such force that the whole thing rocked, slopping undrunk coffee everywhere. With a final glare at Amos, he stormed out of the door, leaving it wide open.

Sam went to close it gently. 'Well, that was good timing.'

'Wasn't it?' agreed Amos. 'I've been

standing outside the door for the last five minutes just to make sure.' He grinned. 'My feet are freezing!'

Sam wiggled his own bare toes. 'Yeah, mine too. I wasn't expecting to have a long conversation when I answered the door. Where have you been anyway?'

'Where do you think?' he said, waving the green sprig in the air. 'It's Mistletoe Day; that stuff doesn't get picked all by itself.'

'You've been out harvesting in this weather? Amos, that's downright dangerous!'

'Well, I wasn't sure you softies would like being turned out of your nice warm beds to come and help. Besides which, I've got nine lives me, and as you can see, I'm perfectly fine. Tradition dictates that the mistletoe is freshly picked for her special day; it's not my place to argue with that. It's all in the barn anyway, plus a little extra surprise.' He winked. 'So when we've had some breakfast, you can give me a hand to bring it in.'

'Ah,' said Sam slowly. 'I think the

agenda for today might have changed a little. I'm assuming you heard some of the conversation with Stephen?'

Amos nodded. 'I did, but that doesn't necessarily change anything. I'm not surprised of course.'

'But it changes everything. Freya will have lost the sale on the house. I know she didn't want to sell it to Stephen, but she did want to sell it.'

'Admittedly, but I wouldn't worry too much if I were you,' he replied, giving Sam a direct stare. 'I had rather thought that she was selling it to both of you as it happens, but it would appear not. That's the only bit I've not quite understood as yet, perhaps you could fill me in.'

'Over a bacon sandwich?'

'That will do nicely.'

* * *

Freya sat on the edge of the bed for a moment, trying to come to terms with quite how late it was, but also the events of the day before, which she was even more unsure how to come to terms with. She hadn't said a word to Sam about the wedding dress, and he hadn't asked her either, just held her close, telling her everything was going to be okay. For quite some time, it felt like it might be, but now in that annoying morning after the night before kind of way, she wasn't so sure. How could it be?

By rights, she should probably be feeling awful. It was a long time since she'd drunk alcohol like that, and mixed with strong painkillers, it was a heady cocktail she had consumed. She was surprised to find, however, that she felt remarkably fine, and even — spurred on by the delicious smell of bacon — ready for an enormous breakfast.

She pulled on her furry slippers and went to see which way the land was lying.

'Aye aye, the boss is up, Sam, more rashers required in the pan,' said Amos, as she walked into the room. 'Good morning, Freya, Merry Mistletoe!'

'Merry Mistletoe, Amos,' she returned. 'I'd forgotten what day it was.' She paused for a moment, head on one side. 'It seems a bit daft I know . . . with everything that's happening, but I wondered if we might bring the mistletoe in today anyway, like we would usually do . . . just for old times' sake.'

'Already taken care of. Sam and I were just going to have some breakfast, and then we're ready to go. It's all in the barn waiting.' He eyed Sam. 'It might still be a bit wet, mind, it's been snowing pretty heavy again this morning.'

She crossed to the window to have a better look, pulling her dressing gown around her a little more tightly. 'Hey, look at that lot. Typical isn't it, the one year there isn't a white Christmas forecast, and it catches us all out.'

Sam cleared his throat. 'Actually, it might not be a bad idea to bring the mistletoe in this year. We might need her help.'

Freya turned to look at him, and tried out a small smile. 'What do you mean?'

'Well, I've just had a rather difficult conversation with Stephen. Perhaps you'd better come and sit down.' He waited until she was seated before pouring her some tea, relinquishing his bacon cooking duties to Amos.

'I probably don't need to bore you with the details as such, I know you're well aware of the things that Stephen gets up to, but I have to admit that his latest escapade is breath-taking even by his standards. I think you should probably give your solicitor a ring, Freya, just to check, but unless Stephen's bank has had a radical change of heart, they aren't going to lend him the money he needs to buy Appleyard.'

She stared at him blankly.

'You're going to lose the sale on the house, Freya,' he added, just in case there was any doubt.

'Yes, I got that,' she replied, feeling her face pale. 'What intrigues me, though, is your use of the possessive pronoun.'

'I'm sorry?'

'*He* needs to buy Appleyard,' she reiterated, 'that's what you said. Things *Stephen* gets up to, *Stephen's* bank.

Where is the 'we' in that statement, only I thought I was selling the house to both of you?'

Amos moved the frying pan off the heat. 'We were just about to have that conversation, Freya,' he said. 'You're lucky you missed Stephen, he was extremely unpleasant. A very foolish, irresponsible young man, and rather manipulative too, I think.'

Freya ignored his intervention. 'So what did he come around for then, Sam? I doubt it was to break the news to me gently. And coming over here in all this snow? Stephen never puts himself out for anyone, so he must have been pretty keen to see someone, and I can only surmise that must have been you.'

'Stephen came around to ask for my help basically, to bail him out of his latest scrape by lending him money so that the sale could continue on this place. I refused.' He swallowed.

'Big of you,' she said. 'I still don't understand.'

'Well, it's not unusual in situations like

this for a mortgage to be raised against one property to help to buy another. That's what Stephen was trying to do. Trouble is that unbeknownst to me, he's already mortgaged Braeburn to help pay off some of his debts, debts which incidentally still exist. The bank won't lend him the money, it's as simple as that. I'm not involved in any of this because I don't own Braeburn, Stephen does.'

Freya stared at him. 'What do you mean you don't own it, since when?'

'Since Dad died and left everything to Stephen.' He held up his hand. 'Hang on, let me finish. What did your dad used to say about mine?'

'He called him a wily old bird, the sharpest business brain around.'

'Exactly, and he was, and he also knew both his sons very well. He called us together a few years before he died to discuss his affairs, and he gave us a choice. He could leave Braeburn to both of us, or only one of us, in which case the other would inherit financially but would never own the orchard. If he left it to both of us, we had to run the business together, and if he left it to only one of us, the other would be granted permission to live there for as long as Braeburn remained in the other's possession. He was giving me an out, Freya.'

Amos placed three plates of sandwiches down on the table. 'As you say, a very astute man.'

'No, I still don't get it. Why would you give all that up, Sam, why let Stephen win?' asked Freya.

'I haven't let him win. Dad knew that Stephen would never want to give up Braeburn, but he also knew that if we had to run the farm together, it would be a disaster. I would have hated it, so he did the best thing he could think of, which was to give me the opportunity to carry on living there but to leave me with an investment that I could use for my own future when the time was right. I think he hoped that Stephen would change his ways and make the best of the opportunity he'd been given too, but he's done exactly what Dad worried he would do.

He's frittered everything away, and now he's lucky if he'll have anything left. I didn't realise it at the time, and I know Dad hoped everything would turn out fine, but he wanted to protect me from going down with the ship. I think I've just realised how astute he actually was.'

'And how much he loved you,' said Amos.

The words hung in the air for a few moments, settling between them all.

'So everything at Braeburn's is Stephen's, the fancy lorry, the posh house, everything?'

'Yes.'

Freya picked at the edge of her cast. 'And Stephen came to you this morning because he wanted to borrow money from you, so he could buy this place?'

'Essentially, yes.'

'And what did you say?'

'I told him no . . . I'm setting myself free, Freya. Finally.'

She considered this for a moment. 'But do you have the money?' she asked quietly.

'It's not what you think, Freya,' he said quickly. 'Please just let me explain.'

'What's to explain, Sam?' she flashed, turning on him. 'I can see exactly how it is. You didn't feel the need to explain any of this before, and I wonder why. Oh, yes, because this is what it's been about the whole time, isn't it? This stupid bloody rivalry between you and Stephen. And now after all these years you've finally got the revenge you've waited so long for. I've been like a lamb to the slaughter, haven't I? You've been keeping me sweet so that you could swoop in at the last minute and buy my house out from under me. Do you even want it, Sam, or is it just to get back at Stephen?' She got up from the table. 'Well, I'll tell you one thing, I'm not going to be piggy in the middle any more. I know what I did was wrong, but I was just beginning to let myself fall in love with you all over again. I didn't realise you still hated me quite as much as you do. You can think again about buying this place, Sam. Over my dead body you will.'

She turned and looked at Amos, the tears spilling from her eyes. 'Excuse me, I need to go and get dressed . . . and you,' she added, pointing a shaky finger at Sam, 'can get out of my house. Now.'

* * *

Sam braced himself for the sound of slamming doors, but none came. Just a deep and all-encompassing silence. He lay his head on the table and groaned. 'As if I couldn't see that coming. It's been inching ever closer, coming at me straight between the eyes, and there didn't seem to be a damned thing I could do to stop it. She's not going to listen to me now, is she? What the hell am I going to do? I can't lose her, Amos, not again.'

Amos laid a hand on his shoulder, and paused for a moment, thinking. He took a deep breath.

'You're going to do what you were going to do before, and that is to help me bring in the mistletoe.'

Sam lifted his head a fraction. 'And

168

that's the sum token of your sage advice, is it?'

'It's very sound advice actually. One, because it will keep you busy for a few minutes, two because it will give Freya the time to fully take in what she's just learned before you go and speak to her, and three, very importantly, because it's Mistletoe Day, and the mistletoe needs to be on the inside, not in the barn.'

'Amos, this is important.'

'Yes, it is, I'm glad you agree. Come on then.'

'I meant . . . this whole thing with Freya.'

'I'm fully aware what you meant,' he replied, not taking his eyes off Sam for a minute.

Eventually, Sam heaved a frustrated sigh, but rose from the table just the same. He stared at Amos, his eyes dark and questioning.

'It will be worth it, Sam, believe me. I'm sure you're well aware of the old-fashioned name for mistletoe. It's not called Allheal for nothing.'

Freya sat on the edge of the bed, cold and numb. She wished with all her heart that she had got it wrong. She had even dared to believe that things could be different after last night, but truly, even after all these years, he still hated her. The thought reverberated around her head. It was all lies, everything he'd done for her these last weeks was all a ruse, all a pretence to soften her up, lure her into a false sense of security before he played his final hand. She knew what she'd done had hurt him terribly, but she'd truly never meant to. She had thought she was in love. At least now she knew where she stood. She had no idea what to do, but she knew that Sam would come and try to talk to her, and she definitely didn't want to talk to him. In fact, there was only one person she did want to talk to. She had to get out of the house.

It was still such incredibly hard work getting dressed, but she pulled on what she could, not caring what she looked like and went softly back downstairs. The kitchen seemed quiet, but she doubled back just the same and went through into the main hallway, pulling open the cloak cupboard quietly and wriggling into the coat that she found there. It was huge on her but meant that at least she could get it around her arm and still button it up. She pulled her red knitted hat on as well and pushed her feet into her boots, opening the front door as quietly as she could. She had no desire to see anyone and instead slipped unnoticed into the white world outside.

The snow was drifting gently down now, small feathery flakes that settled with the lightest touch onto the mounds already there. Snow on snow. She breathed in the cold air deeply, letting it settle around her, and enjoying the sensation. It seemed right to feel cold somehow. She walked down the path and out onto the lane, picking her way carefully through the ruts. She had no idea how long it would take her to walk, but that scarcely mattered; she had all day.

She had always enjoyed walking, loving the way it sent her brain into freewheel. She could surrender to the sheer enjoyment of being outside, putting life into suspended animation until she chose to rejoin the world once again. Thinking only about putting one foot in front of the other had always calmed her and made her feel in control once more, but today even this feeling deserted her. Her head was just as full of white noise as the day outside, and she couldn't make any sense of it.

Their lane turned right onto the main road after about half a mile, and it was trickier here where the snow-plough had gone through. The snow had compacted to ice under its wheels and deep piles of snow had been pushed to the sides of the road. It was safer to walk on the verges — less slippery — but with each step, her foot sank by about twelve inches, and in only ten minutes her legs felt like lead. She stopped for a moment, tears of frustration fuelling the anger that suddenly reared up inside her. She didn't want to turn back, but at this rate she knew she'd never make it to the village either, and she was just about to howl with rage when she heard the rumble of a tractor close by.

She hadn't realised quite how bad the roads were. Even the tractor had found it difficult to navigate at times, but despite the farmer's caution, Freya was still adamant that she wanted to be dropped off in the village. Like most local folk, he'd known Freya most of her life and dressed as she was in her dad's oversized coat, there could only be one place she was headed for today.

The church looked especially pretty with its blanket of snow, the dark yew and holly hedges vibrant under their white topping. A bright wreath adorned the lych-gate and, tucked inside the porch, a Christmas tree twinkled with light. At any other time, Freya would have appreciated its picture-postcard quality. Today the gate creaked fiercely as it opened, but it did so with ease, the path having already been cleared, no doubt in preparation for tomorrow's Midnight Mass. She stepped away from it almost straight away, wading through the thick snow amongst the gravestones.

It saddened her to see the floral tributes half-buried, their colours lost beneath the snow, the weight of it bowing the stems of the roses and chrysanthemums. She crouched beside a grave and lifted the wreath she had placed there over a week ago, its shape only a soft mound in the deep snow. She gently brushed the snow from the greenery, freeing the holly and mistletoe from its cloak and shaking loose what she could. She brought it to her lips for a moment before laying it softly against the icy marble, sweeping the snow from the top of the stone so that none would fall on it.

'Hello Dad,' she whispered.

She hadn't even realised she was crying until a sudden squally gust of wind stung the wetness on her cheeks. She felt hollow inside all over again, just as she had when her dad had died. The last few months had been some of the most painful in her life, but gradually a sense of purpose had filled her, and she had woken each day knowing that, although different, her life was still hers to make of it what she could. She had felt some of her old spirit returning, and each day confirmed what she was beginning to feel: that she would be okay. Now, it felt as though someone had viciously scrubbed out these pages of her life, leaving them obliterated and ragged, the paper torn and scratched so that nothing could be rewritten onto them.

The wind was really beginning to whip up now, blowing white flurries of snow across the graveyard, and she shivered as an icy trickle forced its way down the back of her neck. Her arm was beginning to throb from the cold, and she stood wearily, the stiffness in her legs making her realise just how long she had been crouched there. A robin swooped to perch on the gravestone, its feathers ruffling in the cold wind. It cocked its head to one side, then flew off, landing on a neighbouring stone and immediately swooping away once more. She lost it for a moment before a flash of movement caught her eye. Without thinking she followed it into the church porch where a trug of holly lay next to the Christmas tree. The robin was perched on the handle, a ruby berry held delicately in its beak. It watched her for a moment, its tiny eyes bright, and then flew off once more, leaving a small white feather floating on the wind. In that instant a thought cut through her like a knife.

She saw Sam's face as he had looked in the kitchen that morning, not triumphant as she had thought, but desolate at what he believed he had lost. There was nothing in his expression that had been laughing at her, or smug, or even close to hatred. He loved her, after all this time. He had forgiven her in spite of everything she'd done, and she'd give anything to see him again.

She looked up then, seeing the whiteness outside as if for the first time, and realised that this was no longer the place she should be. She wanted to be among the living. She wanted to be the little robin, who even in the bleakest of times could find what he needed to survive. She pulled her coat around her a little tighter, realising just how cold she was and suddenly scared about how long it would take her to get home.

A jangling noise in the stillness made her jump, echoing around the enclosed porch. She pulled her mobile out of her pocket, trying to hold it with the hand of her injured arm while she frantically tried to remove her glove with her teeth. The ringing went on.

'Hello,' she managed eventually, 'hello.' But the line just crackled as the voice cut in and out. 'Sam,' she tried again, but all she could hear were short bursts of noise and then the line went dead. She stared at her phone. How quickly things had changed. In only a few hours, there was no one else whose voice she'd rather hear.

With shaking hands, she dialled Sam's number, watching anxiously as the snow began to fall thick and fast, but the call went straight to voicemail. As she stared at the display, it suddenly lit up and she jabbed at the accept button, her heart hammering wildly.

'Sam,' she started, her face falling as she realised that he wasn't the caller after all. She was struggling to hear, and moved closer to the edge of the porch trying to angle her body out of the wind and snow that tore at her hair.

The voice cut in loud and clear all of a sudden. 'Merry!' she exclaimed, a smile automatically forming on her lips. 'Oh it's so lovely to hear your voice.' A sudden rush of emotion brought the tears rushing back to her eyes. 'Everything is such a mess, I don't know what to do.' Another thought caught up with her then. 'Oh God . . . how are you? Is it the baby?'

'I bloomin' well hope so, what else could possibly hurt this much?'

'Oh Merry!' said Freya, smiling not at her friend's pain but at her typical matter-of-fact reaction to the things that happened in her life. 'Where are you, at the hospital?'

'No, just about to leave. Tom is doing the whole running-around-in-a-panic thing, and I thought I'd give you a ring to see how everything is. I thought it might take my mind off things, but it seems as if I've rung at just the right time.'

Freya listened to the overly casual tone in Merry's voice, one that Freya had heard her adopt on many occasions over the years. It hadn't fooled her then, and it wasn't fooling her now. 'I see . . . you're sure it's not because Sam has rung you and you're checking up on me?'

There was silence for a moment before Merry heaved a sigh. 'Do you know I thought it might work this time, you know, seeing as we're not face to face, but I can never seem to get one past you, can I?'

'Nope. You never could lie at the best of times. You are actually in labour I suppose? You haven't made that up as well?'

'No, I bloody well have not. I'm in agony here. Listen, Sam's just worried about you, Freya. He couldn't get hold of you, said something about an argument and being out in the snow.'

'We had a fight . . . well not really, but I've done it again, Merry, jumping to conclusions, running off without giving him the chance to explain.'

There was an answering silence. That grew longer. 'Merry?' whispered Freya. 'Are you still there?'

Merry drew in a sharp intake of breath that was readily audible this time. 'Freya . . . I think my waters just broke . . . Oh God, my waters just broke, Freya, I'm going to be a mummy!' Her voice rose with excitement mixed with pain. 'I've got to go, Freya, sorry . . . I'll ring you, okay?'

'Yes, go, go!' replied Freya urgently.

'Listen, just one thing, Freya Sherbourne, and you damn well listen this time,' she panted. 'My whole life is going to change today, nothing will ever be the same again, but it's a good thing. It's the right time for me and if you let it, it can be the right time for you too. Promise me you won't fight what you're scared of, Freya. Breathe through the pain and at the end of it, well you just might have yourself a miracle.'

'Okay.' She nodded. 'I will, I promise.'

She could almost hear her friend nodding, words temporarily deserting her until she got her breath back. 'Good, don't let me down, will you? Okay, I'm going now. Wish me luck . . . '

'Merry Mistletoe!' shouted Freya against the wind, but her friend had already gone. She slipped her phone back into her pocket and, wiping her eyes, set out from the shelter of the porch into the whirling storm. If she was lucky, she would find someone who could take her home.

The church was in the very centre of the village, but even so by the time she had navigated the village green and emerged onto the high street, she was exhausted. The little row of shops huddled together, their twinkly lights shining bravely out into the dimming light, but this was the only sign of the season. The place was deserted; even the butcher's which would usually have a good-natured crowd spilling out onto the street as people queued to collect their turkeys, was eerily quiet. She thought of her own warm house, with its homely kitchen, and roaring fire, fragrant from the apple wood they burned, and her stomach turned over with a tiny shiver of fear. She was finding walking increasingly difficult, her arm still in its sling throwing her off balance, and her wellies, although waterproof, with next to no grip on the snow.

In desperation, she walked towards the baker's at the far end of the street. Millie's husband was a farmer, and it was just possible he might be able to come and collect her. As she walked, she heard a light tinkling noise and then, 'Freya?'

She turned to see the door of the off-licence closing. Stephen stood on the pavement, a carrier bag in his hand. He looked as surprised to see her as she him.

'What are you doing here, Freya? Jesus, you look cold.'

To her further surprise and humiliation, she burst into noisy tears, all her pent-up emotion finally catching up with her.

'You bastard!' she shouted, flailing her arm at him. 'This is all your fault. Why couldn't you just leave me alone?'

Stephen put down his bag on the pavement with a clank, and tried as best he could to get both arms around her as she struggled against him. He said nothing, just tried to calm her, his natural height and build giving him the advantage, and after a while, although the whimpering accusations continued, she eventually stopped wriggling and sagged against him.

'Come on,' he said gently. 'Let's get you home.' He picked up his bag again, and still holding onto her as best he could, moved her slowly down the street to where his car was parked.

'I'm not going anywhere with you,' she sniffed, eyeing his car warily. 'Not if you've been drinking.'

He drew a slow breath in. 'Jesus Freya,'

he said, studying her for a moment, her face a picture of abject misery. 'You really do hate me, don't you? No, don't answer that. I haven't been drinking, not yet anyway. You'll be perfectly safe. Come on, get in.'

He folded her inside, and then set about clearing the windscreen, which even in the short time he had been shopping had completely covered in snow. After a few minutes, he climbed in beside her, and started the Range Rover, turning the heaters up to full.

He was about to put the car into gear, when he suddenly stopped and looked at her.

'Not that it will make any difference to you, but for what it's worth I wanted to say that you're quite right. I *am* a bastard, and it *is* all my fault.'

Freya turned to look at him, sniffing gently, her eyes still full of tears. 'Stop playing games, Stephen, enough is enough.'

'You know, I don't blame you for not believing me, but actually this time, I mean it, Freya, I'm telling the truth. I should never have done what I did. You were young, and I took advantage of that. I knew exactly what I was doing.'

'So why did you then?'

Stephen toyed with the air freshener on the dashboard. 'Because I've always been jealous of Sam, right from when we were children; of the way he made friends when we were young, of the way he made people laugh. Stupid and irrational I know, but there you are. I can't think of one single reason why I should have felt like that, but I did, and anything he had, I set out to take from him . . . including you.'

Freya's lip trembled. 'And I let you take me,' she said sadly. 'I'm just as much to blame.'

Stephen reached for her hand, even now feeling her flinch as he took it. 'No, it wasn't your fault, Freya. I pursued you like a hunter stalks a lion. I showered you with compliments and presents, planted dreams of what our life could be like if we were together, of the riches we would have, the places we would travel to.'

'Empty promises . . .'

'Yes, but you weren't to know that. You were eighteen, not old enough to know what you wanted.'

A tear trickled down Freya's cheek. 'But I did know what I wanted . . . and I let him go.'

The silence stretched out between them for a few minutes, both lost in a time over 15 years ago. 'He wanted to go after you that day, after the wedding, did you know that? But I stopped him. Even then, after all that had happened, he would still have gone after you, but I punched him and knocked him to the ground.'

Freya looked up in shock. 'I never knew that,' she said, her eyes wide. 'But you were angry, Stephen, I'd stood you up in front of all those people. I knew weeks before that I didn't want to marry you, but I let it go too far. I was scared; your dad had done so much, all those beautiful flowers, the marquee, I couldn't bring myself to tell anyone. I just thought I would go through with it and in the end it would all be okay. But on the day . . . I just couldn't . . . I should never have done that either.'

He squeezed her hand. 'We both made mistakes, but I don't blame you for what you did. Marrying me would have been a disaster. I've never said this to you before, but I am truly sorry for what happened.'

Freya looked down at her hands.

'Why are you telling me this now, Stephen?'

'I don't know . . . because it's Christmas . . . because I've fucked up my life and it's time to do something about it . . . because my brother has loved you since primary school and you should be together . . . ' He shrugged. 'I could go on.'

'What will you do?'

Stephen gave a rueful smile. 'Go home and get bladdered one last time and then try to sort my life out. Try to salvage what I can of my home and my business, maybe marry someone like you, try being a grown-up for a change.'

He pushed the gear stick forward. 'But first I'm going to get you home.'

Appleyard was only a three-mile drive from the village, but the snow was coming down so fast now that Freya wondered if they would make it at all. The wind had blown huge drifts against the hedges and in places there was barely room to pass. Even with the car's four-wheel drive, they struggled up the lanes, visibility almost zero, but Stephen drove slowly on, his teeth clenched in his jaw. Freya sat forward in her seat and urged them onwards.

Eventually, the gates to the house came into view and Stephen carefully brought the car to a standstill.

'Are you sure you'll be all right from here?' he asked anxiously.

Freya touched her hand gently to his. 'I will, I'm sure of it.' She leaned over to kiss his cheek. 'And thank you.'

Stephen smiled at her touch, as if in recognition that for once in his life he had done the right thing.

She had only made it halfway up the

drive when the back door opened and a familiar figure half ran, half stumbled towards her. She could feel her heart pounding in her chest as she took the last few steps, until finally she felt Sam's arms go around her and there, swaying gently in his warmth with the snow whirling around them, cold and exhausted, Freya finally came home.

* * *

'I thought I'd lost you again,' murmured Sam as they clung to each other in the quiet solitude of the kitchen. They held each other close, the years catching up with them until a peaceful silence settled on the room, and this was how Amos found them, in a silent embrace, standing oblivious under the mistletoe that they had hung from the rafters only hours earlier. He closed the back door firmly and turned the key in the lock before coming to rest a hand on Sam's shoulder and kiss Freya's cheek.

'Merry Mistletoe,' he whispered.

It was fully dark by the time Freya awoke, stretching luxuriously under the weight of the blankets. After gallons of tea, hot buttered toast and jam and a rather giggly one-armed bath, she'd had no objection at all to being told what to do, and had fallen into a deep sleep.

It was quiet downstairs as she made her way along the landing, pausing for a moment as she spotted Sam sitting at the bottom of the stairs, an open book on his lap. He turned as he heard her footsteps.

'I didn't want to miss you,' he said, holding out his hand and waiting for her to reach his level. 'Come with me.'

She followed his lead along the hallway until he stopped at the door to the lounge. 'Close your eyes,' he instructed, a smile on his face.

She did as she was asked, stepping gingerly into the room, a childlike leap of excitement filling her. The door closed behind her, and she strained her ears, but there wasn't a sound that she could hear.

'Okay you can open them now.'

She peered between her fingers, the room still completely dark, and suddenly she was aware of a familiar fragrance. In the split second that she realised what it was, the room came to life with what looked like a million points of dancing light.

'Oh,' was all she could say, her mouth round as she inhaled a sharp breath of surprise.

In the room before her were a myriad Christmases past; holly and mistletoe heaped along the mantelpiece, woven with tartan ribbons and gilded pine cones, bright red woollen stockings at either end — stockings she herself had knitted. Strings of fairy lights hung across the alcoves on each side of the room, and the edges of the bookshelves were covered in twinkly gold stars. Her patchwork Christmas quilt was thrown over the cream sofa, and the jolly felt reindeer and elves she loved so much stood on the coffee table to one side.

Her gaze swept the room each time seeing something new, but each time coming to rest on the huge tree that stood in one corner, a beautiful spruce of the brightest green and now bearing only the simplest of decoration. As Freya moved closer, something caught in her throat as she realised what was hanging there; each and every one of the beautiful baubles she and her dad had collected over the years, each with its own story to tell and each still as perfect as the day they had bought it. She looked at them all in turn, every one bringing a smile of memory until she saw right near the top, the most recent addition: a shimmering rose globe, caught in the light to reveal its perfect feather frozen in time within. It was utterly, utterly beautiful and left her devoid of words.

She felt an arm go around her, warm and comforting and familiar.

'I thought you might like it,' murmured Sam in her ear. 'It seemed such a shame to leave them in their boxes; all those memories locked away. They need to dance again, don't you think?'

A soft smile lit up Freya's face. 'I think it's the most beautiful thing I've ever seen. When did you do all this?'

'This afternoon while Amos was out looking for you. I wanted to stay here in case you came back, but I had to have something to keep me occupied, I was going out of my mind with worry.'

'I'm so sorry I ran away. I should have let you explain,' said Freya.

Sam placed a finger gently across her lips. 'I seem to remember a time when I should have listened to you, but I let a lot of years go by, letting my stupid pride have its way. We should look to the future now, not the past.'

Freya kissed his fingers, entwining them with her own. 'It was Stephen who brought me home you know. He actually apologised for what happened between us, said it was all his fault. I've carried the guilt of that around with me for so long, Sam.'

'I know.'

'I think he's going to be okay, though, Stephen I mean. He might even be growing up finally.'

Sam smiled, his eyes twinkling in the light. 'Well, it is Christmas, Freya, stranger things have happened.'

She looked at the mistletoe on the mantelpiece, deep in thought. 'Where is Amos by the way?' she asked.

'Gone to bed, he said he'd see you in the morning.' He touched Freya's face once more. 'You know he'll be gone soon, don't you?'

Freya stared wistfully at the bauble on top of the tree, thinking of the man who had come into her life so suddenly and would no doubt leave it the same way. He would remain in her memory for a very long time. 'Yes, I know. He'll go whichever way the wind blows him.'

She watched the light for a moment sparkling on the rose-coloured glass, her eye now drawn to something she hadn't seen before: a bright red velvet box, tied with golden thread.

Sam followed the direction of her

eyes. 'It was supposed to be your Christmas present, but you could have it now if you'd like.'

Freya grinned, trying hard not to jiggle with excitement. Sam lifted the box from the tree, motioning for Freya to come and sit down beside him.

He waited until she had wriggled herself comfortable, sliding onto his knees beside her and drawing a steadying breath. 'Before I give this to you, will you let me tell you what I meant to say this morning? In fact, I should have said this a long time ago . . . I don't blame you for what happened with Stephen, I never did, Freya. I pushed you away as much as he pulled you to him. I'd lived so many years losing things to him, that I viewed it as inevitable in the end. He'd taken so much from me over the years that when I saw him begin to take an interest in you, I thought I never stood a chance. I should have fought for you. What's worse was that I never gave you the opportunity to tell me differently, and I've had to bear the consequence of my stupidity ever since.'

'We're both to blame, Sam. I was flattered by Stephen's attention, and I let myself be seduced by his stupid promises. I knew deep down that he never loved me, but I so desperately wanted to believe everything he told me. I wanted to stay here, among the orchards, to follow in my father's footsteps, raise my own family here. I thought that's what he wanted too, but I knew really it was never the case. Time has shown me that.'

'But is that what you still want, Freya, a life here?'

Her lip trembled. 'More than anything. I thought I could start a new life, buy Merry's shop and move away, be something different, but I can't. This is where I belong. I have to try to find a way to make it work.'

He pressed the box into her hands. 'Open it, Freya,' he said.

She pulled at the thread holding the tiny parcel closed and let it fall away until she was left, with shaking hands, holding the lid. She closed her eyes and opened it.

Inside was a key.

She looked up puzzled for a moment, until it suddenly struck her what it was.

'I'm giving you back Appleyard, Freya, so that you never have to worry about leaving again. The Sherbourne orchard has been here far too long to let it go, I want us to breathe new life into it . . . together.'

'But — '

'I'm asking you to marry me, Freya. To let me live here with you, and work alongside you, as equal partners, 'til death do us part and all that. We can make Appleyard whatever we want her to be, what she deserves to be.'

The clock on the mantel chimed midnight as Freya reached down to pull Sam to her, her lips only inches from his. She smiled softly. 'It's Christmas Eve,' she breathed, 'I wonder what we should do now?'

'Well,' grinned Sam, his lips tantalisingly close to hers. 'I could always help you unpack.'

* * *

In the room, just above them, Amos gave a soft sigh and turned over in his sleep. He pulled the covers a little tighter around him, snuggled into his pillow, and smiled.